"My other anno[...] Ms. Abramson told [...] Jesse Beven's mother [...]

Anthony sat up straight, the bones of his spine suddenly feeling sharp against his flesh.

"Mrs. Beven told me that Jesse has run away," Abramson continued. "I'm sure this news will bring up all kinds of feelings, and I wanted to take the first part of our session to talk about them."

No way. No freakin' way.

Anthony leaned toward Rae, the bones of his back biting into his muscles. "This is crap," he whispered. "Jesse wouldn't bolt. Not without saying something to me."

"So what do you think happened?" Rae whispered back.

"I don't know. But I'm going to find out," Anthony promised.

Don't miss any of the books in this thrilling new series:

fingerprints

fingerprints™

2

haunted

melinda metz

AVON BOOKS
An Imprint of HarperCollins Publishers

Haunted

Printed in the United States of America.

For information address
HarperCollins Children's Books, a division of
HarperCollins Publishers, 1350 Avenue of the Americas,
New York, NY 10019.

 Produced by 17th Street Productions,
an Alloy Online, Inc. company
33 West 17th Street, New York, NY 10011

Library of Congress Catalog Card Number: 00-193285
ISBN 0-06-447266-3

First Avon edition, 2001

AVON TRADEMARK REG. U.S. PAT. OFF.
AND IN OTHER COUNTRIES,
MARCA REGISTRADA, HECHO EN U.S.A.

Visit us on the World Wide Web!
www.harperteen.com

For Liesa Abrams—editor and inspiration

haunted

Chapter 1

Rae Voight's clock radio started blaring. Without lifting her head off the pillow, she reached over and jammed the snooze button.

/I'm watching you, Rae/

Rae scrambled out of bed, her heart scraping up against her ribs. Someone had been in her room. A stranger. The thought she'd picked up when she touched the snooze button didn't feel familiar. It wasn't from her dad. It wasn't from Alice, the woman who cleaned their house. It wasn't from anybody who had any reason to be there.

Okay, okay, she told herself. *First thing you need is information.*

"Come on, you freak, tell me who you are," she muttered. She ran her fingers lightly over the radio,

1

then over her nightstand, including the little lamp.
*/I'm watching you, Rae/***I'm watching you, Rae/***I'm watching you,
Rae/***I'm watching you, Rae/**I'm watching you, Rae/

The thoughts were full of hatred—hatred and fury. She could feel the emotions rush through her body, starting the acid pumping in her stomach, making her knees shake, increasing the temperature of her blood.

No. This can't be happening, Rae thought, her heart now ramming into her ribs. A whole . . . a whole *team* of people couldn't have been in here. It was impossible.

Impossible? Like someone planting a pipe bomb in a bathroom to kill you? Rae asked herself. '*Cause that kind of impossible, it's possible, and you know it.* It hadn't even been that long since it had happened.

Slowly Rae backed way from the nightstand, her eyes locked on it as if it was going to hurl itself off the floor and attack her. She stumbled into her desk chair and grabbed its soft leather back to steady herself.

*/I'm watching you, Rae/I'm watching you, Rae/***I'm watching you, Rae/**

She shoved the chair away from her—
/**I'm watching you, Rae/I'm watching you, Rae/**

—and bolted to the door, then wrenched it open.
*/I'm watching you, Rae/*I'm watching you, Rae/

The hallway was quiet except for the faint sound of Rae's father snoring. She stood perfectly still, trying not to even hear her own breathing. The intruder—no, the *intruders* were gone.

Shower, Rae thought, letting out her breath. Then she could think—really think—about what she should do.

Rae hurried to the bathroom and shoved open the door with her shoulder. She pulled the door closed with two fingers and locked it.

/I'm watching you, Rae/*Watching you!*

Shaking, she switched on the water. These people . . . they had been here, too. Everywhere. What *hadn't* they touched in her home? She stood under the warm spray, the scent of her citrus shower gel filling her nose. She turned away from the nozzle, then leaned back her head and let the water soak her long, curly hair. She'd wash it. Then she'd come up with some kind of—

Rae's eyes locked on the showerhead. There was something glittering behind the dozens of little holes. Every nerve in her body went on red alert. Had they done something to the shower? Was this the second attempt to kill her?

Rae jerked off the water, then pried at the showerhead with her fingernails. She had to get it off, had to see what was under there. One of her nails pulled away from the skin. The pain brought tears to Rae's eyes, but she kept jerking at the showerhead. Finally the part with the little holes came free from the base, and underneath—

"A camera," Rae whispered. She leaned out of the shower and grabbed her toothbrush from the sink.

/Watching you/

Ignoring the thoughts from the brush, Rae used it to stab at the tiny camera lense until it cracked, then she scrambled out of the tub, banging her anklebone on the side and managing to step on one of the pieces of glass.

Damn. Rae grabbed one of the big bath sheets off the towel rack and wrapped it around herself. She needed to do a full-house search for more cameras. But she couldn't walk around leaving a blood trail. She balanced on one foot and pulled the piece of glass free, then opened the medicine cabinet—

/I'm watching you, Rae/

—and screamed. A man was peering at her between the little shelves. He reached through and grabbed her by the shoulders. Shook her.

"Rae," the man exclaimed. He sounded like her father.

Rae's eyes flew open, and she saw her father standing over her, his blue eyes locked on her face. She sat up, pulling free of his grasp.

4

Oh God, it was a dream, she realized, glancing down at the blanket clutched in her hand.

"Sorry. I guess that dream scream came out real, huh?" she asked, trying to sound normal.

"I'll say," her father answered. "It must have been quite a nightmare." He waited, and Rae knew he was expecting her to tell him what it was about. But she didn't want to think about it for even a few seconds more.

"Yeah," she answered. She glanced at her clock radio. 4:01. "But I have time to get in a good dream before I have to get up." She hoped she didn't sound as freaked as she felt. She didn't want her dad to start worrying. For months that's all he'd done—worry about her.

"Let me get you a glass of water," he said.

"That's okay," Rae answered, but he was already out the door. Rae used both hands to shove her hair away from her face. The roots were damp with sweat.

It was just a dream, she told herself. But that didn't make her feel any better. Yeah, it was just a dream. But it was a dream that was all about what she was afraid of in real life. Someone out there wanted her dead. And she had no idea who. Or when they might try again.

Rae's dad hurried back in with the water and pressed the glass into her hand.

/thought she was getting better/

5

"It was just a dream, Dad," she said, wanting him to believe it, even though it wasn't really true. Wanting him to believe that their lives were back to normal, that even though she'd spent the summer in a mental hospital, she was fine, fine, fine. "Just a dream," she repeated, then pulled the covers up as high as she could. But she still felt chilled, as if her spine had turned to ice.

Rae headed toward the cafeteria, trying to exude . . . just your basic normalcy. For years there'd been nothing she wanted more than getting noticed. And she'd done it. She'd been right there in the center, girlfriend of Marcus Salkow, Sanderson's It boy. Then she'd had her little freak-out—make that humongous freak-out—in the caf the day she first started getting the not-her thoughts and she'd been sent off to the walnut farm. Now her biggest ambition was to blend.

Which wasn't all that easy. People were still way too interested in whether or not she was going to have another meltdown to take their eyes off her for long. Rae's steps slowed down. Or did one of them have a different reason for staring? Could one of the people checking her out be the person who wanted her dead? Her eyes jumped from face to face. It seemed ridiculous to think that anyone who went to her school had tried to kill her. They spent all their time planning what to wear and how to get invited to the best parties, and, if they were ambitious, how to get the SAT scores to make it into the college Mom and Dad had their hearts set on. But that was it. Right?

Rae did another quick face scan. When her eyes fell on Jeff Brunner, he blushed the color of an overripe tomato, then lowered his head so he wouldn't have to look at her.

All he needs is a sign that says Kick Me, I'm Scum, Rae thought.

But Jeff wasn't acting all guilty because he'd tried to off her. No, all scum boy had done was decide Rae was such a loser that she'd be *grateful* to let him into her pants. Fortunately Rae'd gotten that piece of info from his fingerprints before Jeff had even gotten close to scoring, and she'd put the little weasel in his place. She watched him scurry into the guys' bathroom like the rodent he was.

It's gonna be a while before he decides to try his luck with another "loser" girl, Rae thought with satisfaction.

She continued down the hallway, almost bumping into a guy who stepped away from the drinking fountain without bothering to look where he was going. "Sorry," he said, turning to face her.

Marcus Salkow. Rae's heart gave a jerk and ended up somewhere in her throat. *The parade of the scum boys continues,* she thought, trying to get a grip.

"Um, how's it going, Rae?" he asked, looking somewhere near her face but not directly at it.

"Fine," she mumbled, heart still slamming around in her throat like a bird that wanted to get out. God, while Marcus couldn't look at her, she couldn't *stop* staring at him. Did he have to be so gorgeous? He was like a poster boy for prep school. A clean-cut, football-player-muscled, blond, green-eyed example of a young southern gentleman. "Fine," Rae muttered again. She continued down the hall, not wanting to drag out the encounter, afraid if she looked at him another second, she'd start drooling or something equally humiliating.

You let him off so easy, she thought. Rae hadn't allowed Jeff to treat her like dirt. Why should Marcus be any different?

Because I loved him, Rae answered herself. *Because I thought he loved me.* Which actually made what Marcus did to her a million times worse.

Without giving herself time to reconsider, Rae spun around and hurried back up to him, ignoring the way her heart now seemed to fill every inch of her body. Pounding, pounding, pounding. "When I said I'm fine, it was true," Rae told him, her words coming out clipped and hard. "Except for the fact that I came back to school and found out that you're with

Dori Hernandez, which no one bothered to tell me." She hauled in a deep, shuddering breath. "Including you."

Marcus didn't answer. He just continued to do that not-quite-looking-at-her thing. Rae took a quarter step to the side, putting herself directly into his line of vision. Her heart-body pounded harder.

"Look. I'm sorry," Marcus finally said. "You were in the hospital, and I didn't think it was a good idea to upset you by telling you . . . you know. I was worried about you." Marcus gave a helpless shrug, then reached out and pushed a lock of her curly hair away from her face. "Really worried," he added softly.

Rae shrank back from his hand. She didn't want him touching her, especially because it still did something to her, started turning her all soft inside. "You were so worried, you never came to visit."

"I came—" he began to protest.

"Once," she interrupted. "People I've barely said hi to came once."

He clicked his teeth together nervously. She'd seen him do the same thing in class when he got called on and didn't know the answer. Rae's heart returned to its usual place in her chest, and the pounding eased up, leaving her feeling numb and hollowed out.

"Rae, it's just that . . ." Marcus's words trailed off.

Before he could start clicking again, Rae jumped in. "Whatever, Marcus. Go find Dori." She turned and walked away. When she reached the cafeteria's double doors, she used her shoulder to open the closest one and slipped inside. She didn't want to hear anyone else's thoughts right now. Her own were more than enough.

She felt a tap on her shoulder and nearly jumped, then spun around.

"Yogurt?" Lea Dessin asked.

Rae's shoulders relaxed. It wasn't her would-be killer—just the best friend who'd totally abandoned her.

"Yogurt," Rae agreed. She didn't have the energy to do anything else.

Lea led the way over to the fro-yo machines, her sleek black hair shining under the fluorescent lights. This felt so normal. But it wasn't. Not anymore. Because now Lea was afraid of Rae. She never said it, of course. And she didn't even really act like it. But Rae knew it was true. Fingerprints didn't lie.

"Do you want to sit?" Lea jerked her chin toward the usual table—correction, what used to be the usual table—as she made her fro-yo sculpture.

She's trying, Rae thought. *Even though she's scared of me, she's trying.*

"Could we maybe be adventurous and—"

"Sit someplace else?" Lea finished for her, still

sounding just a little too peppy. *Clearly overcompensating,* Rae decided as Lea moved out of the way so Rae could get to the frozen yogurt machine.

"Just for today," Rae answered, grabbing a cup and a spoon—new, no prints. She didn't want Lea to think she was going to have to spend all year babysitting her freaky used-to-be best friend. But for this one day it would be so nice just to sit with someone and look normal, a normal girl with a normal friend. No psi power. No streak of insanity. No one out to kill her.

Rae took a napkin out of the metal holder and used it to pull down the handle. "It's always sticky," she explained to Lea as the yogurt spiraled into the cup. God, she wouldn't want to see Lea's expression if she heard the truth.

See, if I touch the handle after you touched it, I'll know your thoughts. And really, I'd rather not. Because you deserve some privacy. And I deserve not to hear how creepy you think I am.

Lea was scared enough already. Hearing the truth would probably send *her* to the funny farm. Ha ha. Hee hee.

"There's a place over there." Lea nodded at a couple of empty seats that were about halfway across the room from the usual table.

"Looks good," Rae answered, leading the way.

She took a seat, and Lea sat down across from her. *Now what?* Rae thought. *What am I supposed to say?* Something nonfrightening. Something normal. But what?

"So, do you already have a ton of homework? I'm buried," Rae said. Pathetic. But at least it was words.

"Yeah, me too." Lea shot a glance over Rae's shoulder.

What is she looking at? Rae wondered. Then she got it. Lea was looking at *the* table, watching Jackie and Vince and Marcus and *Dori*.

Rae got an image in her head of a massive steel door swinging shut, separating her old life—her prehospital, prefingerprint power life—from her new life. Lea was on one side. Lea and Marcus and Vince and Jackie and all Rae's old friends. And Rae was on the other. All alone.

Don't get all soap opera, she told herself. *You're not alone. Dad's on your side of the door. And ... and Anthony Fascinelli and Jesse Beven.* Both the guys from group therapy knew the truth about her psychic ability. Anthony was the one who'd helped her figure out where all the strange thoughts were coming from. And he and Jesse were both okay with it.

And don't forget Yana, Rae reminded herself. Yana Savari had been a volunteer at the hospital.

When she'd asked Rae to exchange numbers, Rae'd thought Yana was just taking her on as a charity case. But Yana was turning into a real friend. A Lea kind of friend, before Lea got all weirded out by Rae.

So get over yourself, Rae thought. She had friends. Maybe not a lot of them—but enough.

"Um, I'm taking chemistry this year, and forget about it. Just the work from that class is killer," Lea said. She took a bite of her yogurt.

Rae took a spoonful of her own. When Lea snuck another glance at her usual table, Rae pretended not to notice. What was the point of making a big deal about it? She and Lea wouldn't be doing this again.

Where the hell is she? Anthony Fascinelli checked his watch. It was still ten minutes before their group therapy session started up. But Rae should be here.

What if whoever had hired David Wyngard to set that pipe bomb and off Rae had already tried again? Or hired someone else to do it? What if she was lying dead somewhere? His stomach did a slow roll. What if—

And then he saw her. Walking across the parking lot like one of those girls in a shampoo commercial, her curly reddish brown hair all bouncy, looking like she owned the world and everyone should just fall at her feet if she smiled at them.

She wasn't being careful. She couldn't look like that—all shampoo commercial girl—and be observing everything that was going on around her. What was wrong with her?

"You're late," Anthony snapped as she approached him. "And you're stupid."

She glanced at her slim silver watch. "I'm early," she corrected him. She didn't bother responding to the stupid part.

"What's been going on the last few days? Have you noticed anything unusual? Have you noticed *anything?*" He wanted to reach out, grab her by the shoulders, and shake her. Instead he jammed his hands in the pockets of his jeans. "Has there been a strange car in your neighborhood? Someone you don't really know trying to get all friendly at school? Someone—"

"A stranger in a van offering me candy if I get inside?" Rae interrupted.

"Is that supposed to be funny?" Anthony demanded. He took a step closer and lowered his voice. "Someone is trying to kill you, remember? I can't believe you're acting like it's all a big joke."

"What do you want me to do? I have no idea who hired David to kill me. Not a clue. Am I supposed to walk around being afraid of everybody? Is that what you want?"

Her voice had this tremor running through it, and

Anthony realized she wasn't all shampoo girl casual. Pretty much the opposite. "I just want you to be safe," he muttered.

"Yeah, well, I want that, too. But it's not like I can be suspicious of the whole world. I'd end up back in the nuthouse," Rae answered.

"We'll figure something out," Anthony said. Although he had no idea how. He shifted from foot to foot, not knowing what to say next. "I guess we should go in," he finally added.

"We're not waiting for Jesse?" Rae asked.

"If we do, we'll all be late, and Abramson will be three times as pissed," Anthony said. He led the way inside and down to the group therapy room. Most of the metal chairs were already filled, but there were two together by the door. He sat down in one, and Rae slipped into the one next to him. He'd feel a lot better if he could keep her this close all the time. Not that he'd be able to do any good if someone came at her with a gun or something.

Ms. Abramson hurried into the room, pulling Anthony away from his thoughts. She shut the door behind her and strode to the center of the circle. She was wearing one of those sleeveless dresses again. Anthony figured she had to lift weights because her dark arms were all muscle, none of that jelly at the tops like a lot of women her age had.

"I have a couple of announcements before we start," Abramson said. She flipped one of her many braids over her shoulder. "First, Anthony Fascinelli was not responsible for the pipe bomb. I'm sure you all heard that Mr. Rocha found materials for a bomb in Anthony's backpack, but they were put there by David Wyngard. Obviously David will no longer be a member of our group." She turned her gaze to Anthony, her eyes bright with emotion. "On behalf of Mr. Rocha and me, I want to apologize for making a judgment too quickly and to welcome Anthony back."

Yeah, right, Anthony thought. He could believe Abramson felt bad and wanted him back in group. But there was no way the director of the institute was all happy Anthony was back at Oakvale. Rocha'd been totally psyched to have a reason to give Anthony the boot.

Abramson began to pace back and forth across the center of the circle. "My other announcement is a disturbing one. I got a call from Jesse Beven's mother."

Anthony sat up straight, the bones of his spine suddenly feeling sharp against his flesh.

"Mrs. Beven told me that Jesse has run away," Abramson continued. "I'm sure this news will bring up all kinds of feelings, and I wanted to take the first part of our session to talk about them."

No way. No freakin' way.

Anthony leaned toward Rae, the bones of his back biting into his muscles. "This is crap," he whispered. "Jesse wouldn't bolt. Not without saying something to me."

"So what do you think happened?" Rae whispered back.

"I don't know. But I'm going to find out," Anthony promised.

Chapter 2

All right, it's time for Rae and me to play a game. The name of the game is: What Power Does Rae Voight Have? It's been harder than I thought to learn the truth about Rae. She doesn't open up easily, hides what she's thinking and feeling. But with my game, it won't take long to find out everything I want to know. And after I do, it will be time for Rae to pay—pay for everything that's been taken from me.

* * *

Rae headed toward the exit leading to the school parking lot. She heard footsteps behind her, and her breathing started coming a little faster.

Get a grip, she told herself. *Of course you hear footsteps behind you. There are people everywhere.* She sped up, anyway. The footsteps sped up, too.

Someone was keeping pace with her. *Okay, when you get to the parking lot—*

"Rae, can I talk to you for a minute?"

Rae whirled around and saw Mr. Jesperson. Her breathing returned to normal. The expression on Mr. Jesperson's face told her exactly what he wanted to talk to her about. And it definitely wasn't what book she planned to write her English paper on. No, he wanted to see how she was *doing*.

"I just wanted to check in, see how you're doing," he said when he reached her.

God, this must have been on the agenda at the last teachers' meeting, Rae thought. *Item 1: Everyone make sure Rae Voight isn't about to do another public freak-out.*

She forced a smile. "I'm doing good. Still going to group, which is helping." That wasn't exactly true, but it was what Mr. Jesperson wanted to hear—what they all wanted to hear.

He nodded, and Rae expected him to walk away, having done his good deed for the day. That was what usually happened. But Mr. Jesperson took a step closer, proving he had no clue about the meaning of personal space. "I know I wasn't around last year when you started, uh, having some troubles. But I want you to know that you can talk to me. Just come on in my classroom. Whenever."

Rae knew that a lot of girls thought Mr. Jesperson was a total hottie with his black hair and that trace of stubble he always had going. But he was kind of giving her the creeps. She wished he'd back up, even just half a step.

"I'm doing okay. Really. Thanks, though." She took a step away, hoping it looked casual and not scared-bunny-ish.

Mr. Jesperson moved closer. This time Rae didn't allow herself to back away. "When I was in college, I went through a bad stretch," he confessed, his voice dropping lower. "I almost flunked out. I was pretty messed up there for a while. So don't think if you did decide to talk to me that I wouldn't understand."

"Thanks," Rae repeated. "I've gotta go. I'm meeting a friend."

"Good. That's good. Friends are really important," Mr. Jesperson said. "Go on. I'll see you in class."

"See you," Rae answered. And she was outta there, down the hall and out the exit that led to the parking lot. She scanned the cars—lots of Beemers, a couple of Range Rovers, and a bunch of other SUVs—looking for Anthony's beat-up Hyundai. Well, actually, Anthony's mom's beat-up Hyundai. Not there yet. And he'd given *her* grief for being late yesterday. Although that was just because he was worried about her. Even without all her therapy, she wouldn't have had a problem making that diagnosis. Rae smiled. She wondered if Anthony knew he had marshmallows for guts.

A horn honked to her left, and she turned, expecting to see Anthony, who was definitely the kind of guy who would just honk and wait for her to come running. Instead she saw Yana's yellow Bug zipping in her direction. Yana screeched to a stop next to Rae, then leaned her head out the window, her white blond hair almost covered by a baseball cap, and grinned. "You up for the Underground? If I don't get to a mall in the next half hour, I'm going into withdrawal. Not that I have any money to shop with. But still."

Rae shook her head. "Sorry. I can't today. I'm meeting someone."

"Someone," Yana repeated with a sly smile, clearly having broken the code that *someone* equaled *guy.* "Can't you even remember his name? I mean, I know prep school boys are made from cookie cutters—all clean-cut and white teeth. But I thought, you being a prep school girl, you'd at least be able to tell them apart even if I can't."

Rae wondered what Yana would think of Marcus. He *was* kind of cookie cutter, except he was the cookie all the other guys wanted to be like.

"So can I meet him?" Yana asked. "I could stash the

car on the street. I know that you probably don't want to be seen with someone who actually drives a Bug."

"It *is* pretty humiliating," Rae answered. It felt so good to be with someone who treated her like a normal person, who didn't seem to think she had to be careful of every word that came out of her mouth. "But don't stress about it," she continued. "The guy I'm meeting drives a Hyundai." She didn't bother pretending the someone wasn't a guy. Clearly she was busted.

"You're blowing me off for a Hyundai driver?" Yana cried, her blue eyes narrowed in mock anger.

"It's Anthony," Rae explained. "The guy who got framed for that pipe bomb—the one you helped me clear. And we're not going to be having *fun* or anything. We're meeting with the mother of this kid from our group who supposedly ran away."

Why did I tell her that? Yana knew Rae'd been hospitalized over the summer. She not only knew it, she'd seen it up close and personal when she was volunteering. But Rae didn't need to remind Yana that she was still doing group therapy. It was way too hospital-esque.

"Supposedly?" Yana asked.

Rae shrugged. "I don't know him that well. But Anthony does, and he doesn't think that's what happened. And he thought, um, it might help to have a

23

girl be there when he talked to the mom, that it might make her more comfortable or something." She definitely wasn't telling Yana that she was going to do a fingerprint search. Yana might not freak. She might be totally cool about it, the way she was about Rae's mental health history, but Rae just didn't want to risk it.

"I guess helping out a friend is a decent reason to pass on the shopping. But you have to promise to go with me later this week," Yana said.

"How about Saturday?" Rae suggested.

"I'll pick you up in the morning," Yana volunteered. "I want to get there right when the stores open." She glanced in the rearview mirror. "Hyundai alert." She leaned closer to the mirror, her nose almost touching it. "He's pretty cute, if you like that bad boy look."

Anthony gave an impatient double honk. "Go," Yana told her. "I don't need to meet him. I know the type. And you guys have a mission. See ya later." She lurched toward the exit, tires squealing.

Rae headed over to Anthony's car, but not too fast. That double honk was borderline obnoxious, and she wasn't going to reward him by scurrying over. She opened the door and climbed in.

Weird. She didn't get any thoughts off the door handle. She should have picked up at least one or even the static that came when there was a bunch of old fingerprints.

"I can't start driving until you shut your door," Anthony told her.

Rae slammed it. No thoughts from the inside handle, either. "Did you clean the car before you picked me up?" she asked.

"Does it look clean?" he asked, nodding at the jumble of fast-food wrappers on the floor.

"I meant the handles," she said.

Anthony didn't answer right away. He acted all caught up in maneuvering the car out of the parking lot and heading for the closest freeway entrance.

"Yeah," he finally muttered, sounding embarrassed.

"It's okay," Rae told him. "I have a lot of thoughts I wouldn't want anyone to know."

"You probably *get* a lot of thoughts you don't want to know, too," he answered. "It's not like people walk around thinking about kittens or stuff like that."

Rae shrugged. "A lot of what I get is just routine, you know? Like thoughts about having to study for a test or what to eat for lunch. But yeah, some are . . . some I'd be perfectly happy not to hear." Like the ones about what a freak she was. Her first day back at school she'd gotten a bunch of them. There were fewer now, but she could still be walking around, minding her own business, and—wham—get hit with one. And it wasn't only the ones about her that sucked. Sometimes she got thoughts from total strangers about other total strangers that were so full of rage or jealousy or fear that they made Rae dizzy.

"So, does Mrs. Beven know we're coming?" Rae asked, shifting in the seat.

"I called her yesterday after group. She's up for it. I think she's hoping Jesse will get in touch with me," Anthony answered. He pulled onto the highway entrance and merged into traffic in one smooth motion. *Definitely not a Yana-style driver,* Rae thought.

"So, you're pretty positive that Jesse didn't run away," Rae said.

"Not without saying something to me," Anthony replied.

She'd already known the answer, but she'd felt like she had to keep the conversation going. It was still weird being with Anthony outside of group or the juvenile detention center where she'd visited him after he was framed for the pipe bomb.

You helped get him out, too, she reminded herself. But she still felt guilt-coated when she thought about it. Just slimy.

"And he didn't even hint or anything?" Rae asked. As soon as the words came out of her mouth, she felt like an idiot. If Jesse had hinted, Anthony would have told her. Now it seemed like she didn't trust him or something. Like she was interrogating him.

"He just acted the way he always does. Didn't even mention a fight with his mom or anything," Anthony answered. Rae darted a glance at him. He didn't look annoyed. Just tense, his hands locked on the wheel so tightly that the veins were standing out.

He's only halfway hearing what I'm saying, Rae thought. *He's obsessing about Jesse.* She didn't have to be a fingerprint reader to know that. Rae decided to give him a break and just shut up. He didn't need lame attempts at conversation.

They rode in silence until Anthony turned onto a street in a shabby neighborhood full of ragged lawns and houses with flaking paint jobs. "Jesse's is at the end of the block," Anthony said.

"Have they lived here long?" Rae asked.

"About a year. Since they moved to Atlanta," Anthony said as he pulled into the driveway and parked.

"So you guys haven't known each other that long?" Rae was surprised. Jesse treated Anthony like a big brother. And Anthony let him. She figured they'd known each other for years.

"About eight months, I guess." Anthony climbed out of the car and slammed the door. Rae was right behind him, picking up one of her own thoughts off the clean door handle.

/ Yana's right /

Anthony led the way up to the door and rang the bell. Mrs. Beven answered almost before he pulled his finger away, clearly she'd been watching for them. "Come on into the kitchen," she said, her words coming out too fast, almost running into each other. "I made cinnamon cookies. I hope you like them. About halfway through I realized I should have made chocolate chip."

"I love cinnamon," Rae assured her.

"Sounds great," Anthony added.

"It's right back here," Mrs. Beven told them, heading into the house with jerky little steps.

I never would have pegged her as Jesse's mom, Rae thought as they followed Mrs. Beven. It wasn't just that Mrs. Beven had dirty blond hair while Jesse's was screaming red. Or that she had brown eyes while Jesse's were bright blue. It was more an attitude thing. Jesse was so high-energy, always excited about something or pissed off, willing to talk to anybody. His mom was high-energy, too, but in a totally different way, like she was so nervous, she had to be in motion all the time or she'd start screaming. And Rae got the feeling that Mrs. Beven would rather not talk to anyone if she could help it.

"Sit, sit," Mrs. Beven said when they reached the

kitchen. Rae took the chair closest to the window. It had plastic strips for the seat and back, and Rae realized that Jesse and his mom were using backyard barbecue furniture in the house.

"Go ahead and take the cookies," Mrs. Beven said, hurrying over to the fridge. "And tell me what you want to drink. We have cola, orange juice, milk, and water, of course."

"Milk, please," Anthony said from his seat next to Rae.

"Me, too," Rae added. She took a cookie off the plate in the middle of the table. Anthony grabbed a couple, then he gave Rae a look that said, Go ahead and do what you're here to do.

Rae'd been planning to wait a few minutes at least, have a cookie, make some chitchat. But whatever. She put her cookie down on the little flowered saucer in front of her. "Um, would you mind if I used the bathroom?" she asked Mrs. Beven.

Mrs. Beven turned around so quickly, she almost spilled the two glasses of milk she was holding. "Of course. I should have offered. You go back past the front door and down the hall. It's the first door on the left."

"Be right back," Rae said. She followed Mrs. Beven's directions, then kept on going. She tried the second door on the left.

/where is he?/

Rae felt a lump form in her throat as the thought and static blast behind it hit her. The thought and the salty ball of unshed tears were clearly Mrs. Beven's. And so was the room. Jesse would never stand for a lavender bedspread. There was only one more door in the short hallway, right across from Mrs. Beven's. Rae opened it—

/maybe I could trade my/

—and ducked inside. Yep, it was Jesse's. You couldn't even see the paint on the walls. They were covered, top to bottom, with pages from skateboard magazines and comic books.

"Okay, Jesse, what do you have to say for yourself?" Rae whispered. She turned around and lightly ran her fingers over the inside doorknob.

/can't believe X-Files/over in Little Five Points/Mom's sleeping all/that math test/

Emotions flicked through Rae. Irritation, anticipation, worry, anger. But none of it felt intense enough to be a trigger for Jesse running away.

She scanned the handles of Jesse's dresser next. Same deal. Some frustration about his mom. Some hostility about someone Rae thought was a teacher. Some excitement about a new comic book. A fragment of a plan to meet some guys at the skateboard park. But nothing that gave her any reason to think he was planning to take off.

Closet door handle next, she thought. But it was a bust, too. All she really got was the fact that Jesse was not a morning person. Rae opened the closet and peered inside. It was surprisingly neat. Some clothes. A couple of pairs of shoes. A stack of comics, each in a plastic sheath. A baseball bat. She checked the comics—and got thoughts about comics. She checked the bat—and got thoughts about baseball.

Rae closed the closet and scanned the room. She decided to touch the window frame next. If Jesse ran away, maybe he snuck out through the window.

/no air-conditioning/got to ask Mom/set alarm/friggin' paper route/

Nothing, Rae thought as the static buzz faded. It wasn't like Jesse would run away because he didn't like his paper route. She wanted to do a few more fingerprint sweeps, but she was worried that Mrs. Beven would come and check on her if she was gone much longer. It seemed like something she would do.

If he was really upset about something, I would have picked it up on one of the places he touches a lot, like the doorknobs, Rae told herself. Because if things were so bad, he wanted to bolt, he'd be thinking about it practically all the time. She hurried out of the room, letting the thoughts and feelings from the doorknob flow through her again, and returned to the kitchen.

"So there's no place that you can think he might be?" Mrs. Beven was asking Anthony.

"I can ask around. I know some of his friends," Anthony said as Rae sat back down.

"That would be wonderful. I'm so worried about him," Mrs. Beven said. She picked up the glass of water in front of her and took a long swallow. "You know he's run away before. But I thought things were better. Didn't you?" She reached out and covered one of Anthony's hands with her own.

"I did," Anthony told her. He gave Mrs. Beven's hand a squeeze, and Rae was struck again by what a decent guy Anthony was under his bad boy attitude. "Um, I was wondering if Jesse took any stuff with him," Anthony said. "That might say if he was planning to be gone long."

He doesn't want to tell her he thinks something else could have happened to Jesse, Rae realized. *He's probably right. It would completely freak her out.*

Mrs. Beven took another long swallow, draining her glass. "I checked, but it didn't look like he took anything. I wish he had. He might get cold or . . ." She let her sentence trail off.

Rae believed Mrs. Beven was telling them everything she knew, but just in case—

"Do you have any ideas of places Anthony and I could check?" she asked. "We'll go anywhere you say."

Mrs. Beven picked up her glass again, then realized it was empty and put it down. "You two would know more than I do," she admitted.

Rae jumped up from her chair. "Let me get you some more water," she volunteered. She snatched up the glass before Mrs. Beven could protest.

/oh God/his father/what if/wrong cookies/doesn't know where/his father/what if his father took him/

The glass slipped out of Rae's hand, her fingers suddenly feeling limp and nerveless. Her legs, too. Any second they were going to buckle. Rae stumbled to the counter and braced herself with both hands.

/should have gotten 7UP/Jesse wouldn't/his father/

"Are you okay?" Anthony demanded.

"I just got a little dizzy for a second," Rae answered. The fear that wasn't her own slowly faded, and the strength returned to her body. She turned around and forced herself to smile at Mrs. Beven. "I guess I need one of your cookies. It will get my blood sugar up."

Rae started for her chair, then paused to pick up the glass she'd dropped. At least it hadn't broken.

"No. Let me, let me," Mrs. Beven exclaimed. Rae obediently sat down. She could tell Anthony was going nuts trying to figure out what had just happened. "Later," she mouthed at him.

Rae took a cookie and choked it down, still feeling a little queasy. God, the fear she'd gotten from touching Mrs. Beven's fingerprints had been almost overwhelming. Rae didn't want to do anything to make Jesse's mom feel even worse. But there was a question she had to ask. She waited until Mrs. Beven was sitting down again.

"Do you think that Jesse's dad might have any idea where he could be?" she blurted out.

Mrs. Beven immediately jumped back up, grabbed a dish towel, and started wiping off the table, her motions abrupt and clumsy. "Jesse hasn't seen his father since we moved here. He wouldn't know how to find Jesse even if he wanted to, which he doesn't."

But she's afraid his father took him. I know it, Rae thought.

"We should probably get going," Anthony said.

"Yeah," Rae agreed. It was clear that they weren't going to get any more info from Mrs. Beven. "We'll let you know if we find out anything."

"What exactly happened in there?" Anthony asked as soon as he and Rae were back in the car. He stuck the key in the ignition but didn't turn it. "You looked like you were about to faint or something."

Rae shoved her curly hair away from her face with both hands. "When I touched Mrs. Beven's glass, I got so scared. I knew I was safe, just standing in the kitchen. But I could hardly stand up, I was that terrified."

"You got a thought about Jesse's dad, right?" Anthony asked. "That's why you asked about him."

"Yeah. A bunch of thoughts about him, actually," Rae answered. "The worst one was, 'what if his father took him.' The emotion that came with that one. Whoa."

A flicker of motion in the kitchen window caught Anthony's attention. "We should leave. Jesse's mom is probably wondering why we're still here. In another second she'll be making us chocolate chip cookies or something." He reached for the key, then hesitated. "Are you okay to go? I mean, are you still dizzy?" He couldn't shake the image of her in the moment she dropped that glass. It was like she wasn't even Rae anymore. Like all the life got sucked out of her. And he was powerless to do anything about it.

"I'm good. It doesn't last that long. That one was just intense," Rae answered.

Anthony started the car and backed out of the driveway. "I guess you don't know the deal about Jesse's dad," he said. "He beat up Jesse's mom a lot. Sometimes Jesse. This one time he half-killed her, and a nurse at the hospital hooked them up with one of those women's shelters where they help you move and change your name and stuff."

"God," Rae said under her breath. Anthony shot a

glance at her. She was staring straight ahead, a tiny furrow between her eyebrows. "So Jesse's dad really doesn't know where they are, like Mrs. Beven said?" Rae asked.

"He shouldn't. But who knows? Jesse tracked him down on the Internet. I guess it made him feel better knowing exactly where the guy was. He works at a bar in New Orleans."

"Jesse's never tried to contact him, though?"

"No friggin' way. He only wanted to know where the guy was so he could make sure that he and his mom stay far enough away," Anthony answered.

"I can see why Jesse's dad snatching Jesse is the worst thing Mrs. Beven could imagine," Rae said. "But it doesn't seem that likely, does it?" She reached over and popped open the glove box. "Hey, I remember this. We had this workbook in my fourth-grade class. Is it your little sister's?"

Anthony's veins caught fire. Rae's fingers were an inch away from his English workbook. *His.* If she touched it, she'd know he was a total moron.

"What the hell are you doing?" He grabbed the workbook and hurled it into the backseat, then slammed the glove box shut, almost catching one of her fingers.

Rae's eyes widened. "I was about to look for a piece of gum because drinking milk always leaves this icky coating in my mouth," she explained, looking at him like he'd grown two heads.

"It's out of line to go rifling through someone's stuff," Anthony snapped, even though he knew he should be apologizing.

"Oh, and it's not out of line to practically chop off my hand," Rae muttered.

They rode for a minute in charged silence.

"It's the fingerprints thing again, right?" Rae finally asked. "You cleaned off the door handles, but you didn't clean inside the glove compartment." She shook her head. "I'm sorry. I'm not trying to . . . to *spy* on you. It's just that it's pretty hard to remember that I can't touch anything."

"It's no biggie. I was an idiot," Anthony said. He opened the glove box, rooted around until he found a box of his mother's Tic Tacs, and tossed them in her lap.

"Thanks." Rae took one and then shook the box at him.

He held out his hand to take one, even though he didn't really like them. "So what were you saying? Before, you know." *Before you almost found out how freakin' stupid I am,* he added silently. He'd told Rae once, who the hell knew why, that he was in a slow learner class. But that wasn't the same as her knowing that he was using the same workbook she used in the fourth friggin' grade.

"Um, I was saying that it didn't seem that likely Jesse's dad took him," Rae answered.

"One way to find out," Anthony answered. "You see a pay phone anywhere?"

Rae dug around in her purse. "I have my cell," she said, pulling it out.

A cell. Of course a girl like her would have a cell phone.

"See if you can get the number for a place called Hurricanes in New Orleans."

"Got it," Rae said a few moments later.

"Will you dial it for me?" Anthony asked.

She punched in some numbers and gave him the phone. It felt too small in his hand, kind of like a doll thing. A woman answered on the third ring.

"Hey," Anthony said. He wasn't sure how loud he needed to talk since the mouthpiece wasn't anywhere near his mouth, but from the look Rae was giving him, not as loud as he'd thought. He lowered his voice a little. "I'm a friend of Luke Gilmore's. I wanted to surprise him this weekend. Does he still work there?"

"Saturday through Thursday night," the woman said.

"Cool. Thanks." Anthony didn't even attempt to hang up the phone. He just thrust it back at Rae. "We're going on a road trip to New Orleans this weekend," he told her.

Chapter 3

Rae pulled a folded pajama shirt out of her dresser, then hesitated before putting it in her gym bag. Should she bring it? Why hadn't she asked Anthony if they were staying over? Wouldn't they have to stay over? It was, like, eight hours to New Orleans, plus time in the bar. They wouldn't try to drive back tonight, would they? Especially because Rae didn't have her license yet and couldn't help with the driving.

She shoved the sleep shirt in the bag. If she needed it, she'd have it. *Yeah, now you just have one other teeny, tiny little thing to do before you go,* Rae told herself. *Tell Dad . . . something.* Which she should have done Thursday night. Or Friday morning. Or at least Friday night. But she couldn't come up with the right lie. Maybe there was no right lie that would get any dad to give permission for his daughter to go to New Orleans with someone he didn't even know, less than a month after she got out of the nuthouse.

"Okay," she whispered. "Okay. Here goes. Dad, I . . . Dad, I . . ." Hopeless. Totally hopeless. She opened her mouth to try again.

The doorbell rang. "That better not be Anthony," Rae muttered. He wasn't supposed to be there until eleven. She sprinted for the door. If it was Anthony, she wanted to get to him first. She yanked open the door. "Yana. It's you."

"Got it on the first try," Yana answered. "Ready to shop?"

Rae winced. "Oh God. I totally forgot. I'm losing my mind." She and Yana both cracked up. "My brain," Rae corrected herself. "I'm losing parts of my brain, like the part that remembers stuff. I'm not going insane again."

"But even though you forgot, you still want to go, right?" Yana asked.

Rae frowned. "Wrong. Sorry. The thing is—" She glanced behind her, doing a Dad check. "Remember that kid I told you about? The one who might have run away? Well, there's a chance his father snatched him. Anthony and I are going to go check it out. If I can come up with a good enough story to feed my dad, that is."

"Tell him you're going shopping with me," Yana suggested.

"Problem. The guy's in New Orleans. I don't think I'll be back until tomorrow," Rae said.

"Let me handle this," Yana said. She'd been wearing her Hawaiian shirt knotted above her stomach, but she quickly undid the knot and smoothed the shirt down over her hip-hugging pink vinyl pants, covering up the DNA-strand tattoo that circled her belly button. "Okay, now, where's Dad?"

"He's in his study," Rae answered.

"Take me," Yana instructed, giving her collar-length blond hair a little fluff with her fingers.

Rae wasn't sure this was the best idea. But she had to do *something*. Anthony was going to be there in less than an hour. She led the way to the study, gave a quick knock, then stepped inside, Yana right behind her. "Dad, you remember Yana, right? From the hospital?"

A flicker of pain crossed her father's face at the word *hospital,* then he stood up, reached across his desk, and shook Yana's hand. Actually shook her hand. He was such a dork sometimes. "Of course I remember," he said. "I really appreciate what a friend you were to Rae in there," he told Yana.

"Now it's me who needs a friend," Yana said. "See, my father has this business dinner in New Orleans tonight, and he's dragging me along. But I don't want to sit in a hotel all by myself, so I came over here to beg you to let Rae come with us. We'll be back tomorrow."

"I think that sounds wonderful. You'd like to go, wouldn't you, Rae?" her father asked.

Rae blinked. "Um, y-yeah, of course I want to go," she stammered. She couldn't believe he'd given permission so easily. *Yana comes through again,* she thought. *What would I do without that girl?*

"Thanks so much, Mr. Voight. We have to get going right away," Yana said.

"I'll just quickly pack some stuff," Rae added. It wouldn't look good if her dad knew she'd packed before Yana asked.

"I'll help you." Yana pulled Rae out of the study, and they rushed down the hall to Rae's room. Rae shut the door behind them. "Oh my God. You were brilliant."

Yana retied her shirt below her chest. "Of course I was." She smiled at Rae. "Do you have any clothes I can borrow?"

"Sure. Like what kind?" Rae asked.

"New Orleans clothes, baby," Yana answered. "You don't think I'm staying home, do you?"

"Stop here!" Yana ordered, giving Anthony a whack on the shoulder from the backseat. "We need snacks for the road."

He couldn't believe this girl. She shouldn't even be on this trip, and now she was trying to boss him around. "We don't have time," he told her.

"Oh, come on. It'll take two seconds," Yana protested. "You want snacks, don't you, Rae?"

You better not say yes, Anthony thought. *It's your fault I have to deal with her.*

"Sure," Rae answered. "Snacks would be good."

"Fine," Anthony muttered. He pulled into the Quick Stop lot and snagged a space almost right in front of the door.

"You guys wait here," Yana told them. "I'll get the stuff."

As soon as she'd gotten out of the car and slammed the door behind her, Anthony turned to Rae. "What is she doing here?"

"She's the one who convinced my dad to let me come," Rae answered.

"And?" Anthony said.

"Look, she really helped me out when I was trying to get enough evidence to prove that David set the pipe bomb and not you," Rae explained. "It's a good thing she's with us. You'll see."

Anthony snorted. What other response was there? "At least she didn't lie about only taking a minute," he said, spotting Yana getting in line to pay.

"Um, Anthony, she doesn't know about the

fingerprint thing, and I don't want her to, okay?" Rae blurted out.

"Oh, you mean it's supposed to be a secret?" Anthony asked sarcastically. What did she think he was? An idiot?

"I just thought since Yana and I are friends, you might assume she knew," Rae answered. "And, um, I also wanted to tell you that you don't have to worry about me accidentally getting your thoughts anymore. I bought this stuff called Mush. You put it on dogs' paws when it's hot or when it's snowing, and—"

"What are you talking about?" Anthony interrupted.

"It's basically wax," Rae explained. "I put it on my fingers so I wouldn't pick up anything." She waved her fingers in front of his face. They looked a tiny bit shinier than usual, but that was it. "I'll wipe it off when—" Rae stopped abruptly as Yana climbed back in the car.

"Okay, who wants what?" Yana asked as Anthony pulled back out into traffic. "I got your Snowballs. I got your beef jerky. I got your Cheese Waffies. I got your M&M's—plain, peanut, and crispy. I got your Corn Nuts."

A road trip with a girl who's in love with the sound of her own voice. Excellent, Anthony thought. From the second he saw her, he'd known Yana would be a pain in the butt. Girls didn't dress the way she did unless they wanted attention—a lot of attention. And girls who wanted a lot of attention were always a pain in the butt. If you gave them some, they wanted more. If you didn't, they got all pouty. He couldn't believe Rae and this Yana chick were friends.

"So, how do you two know each other, anyway?" Anthony asked.

"What, you don't think I go to Sanderson Prep?" Yana replied, fingering one of the four earrings she had in her left ear.

"Well, do you?" She wasn't his idea of a prep school girl. But what did he know? It wasn't like he hung out with hordes of them or anything. Rae was pretty much the only one he'd ever talked to.

"No, Rae and I . . ." Yana hesitated. Anthony glanced in the rearview mirror and caught Yana looking at Rae, as if she was waiting for Rae to tell her what to say. What was the deal there?

"Yana was a volunteer at the hospital where I was, uh, *vacationing* this summer," Rae finished for her. She turned her head and stared out the window.

Nice work, Anthony, he told himself. Now Rae'd probably spend the rest of the trip thinking about how it felt to be institutionalized.

"You should have seen the place," Yana said. Anthony shot her a glare in the rearview mirror. But either she didn't see him, or she just blew him off.

"The doctors and the nurses, they were as freaky as the patients. Remember the wig lady, Rae?"

Rae laughed. A real laugh, not one of those fake ones people used to show that they weren't bugged by some stupid thing someone just said. "The wig lady was this nurse who had pulled out most of her hair, strand by strand," Rae explained. "She had a different wig for every day of the week. And she really believed that people thought it was her hair."

"It's called trichto something, when you pull out your hair like that. I can't remember exactly," Yana jumped in.

"Yana's the one who found out what the deal was. She was always calling up personnel files on the computer and then telling all of us really personal stuff—like who'd taken a leave of absence to go into rehab for coke addiction," Rae explained. "Did you know there's a rehab place just for medical people druggies?"

"I only did it because I didn't think it was fair that all the info went one way. Like, why should some doctor get to know everything about Rae's childhood but not have to ever say anything about himself?" Yana asked.

"Oh my God. You should have seen these puppet shows Yana would put on," Rae said, struggling to talk around her giggles. "We had these puppets that we used for therapy sometimes, and Yana would put on soap operas with them, using all the staff people as characters."

"That's cool," Anthony said. And he actually meant it. Maybe it wouldn't totally suck having Yana along on this trip.

Rae glanced over her shoulder. Yana was zonked out, with her head pillowed on Rae's gym bag. "She's asleep," she told Anthony, careful to keep her voice low.

"I figured," he answered, his voice soft, too. "Either that or she fell out of the car. It's been way too quiet from back there."

He sounded more amused than annoyed. Rae smiled as she leaned the seat back and stretched her legs out in front of her. The Yana magic had already started working on Anthony. It was pretty much impossible not to like the girl—unless you were a nurse whose personnel file she happened to have hacked her way into.

Rae rolled the window down a little more, pulled in a deep breath of the warm, moist air, and stared out at the dark highway ahead of them.

"What was it like in there? In the hospital?" Anthony asked. "You don't have to talk about it if you don't want to," he added quickly.

Rae let her eyes drift shut. She saw her hospital room with its two single beds, her roommate pretty much always asleep unless one of the nurses forced her to participate in one of the activities.

"The place was okay," she said. "Except the smell. Way too much disinfectant. But I didn't know about the fingerprints thing. I was sure I was going crazy, and I was so afraid I was going to die in there, like—" She stopped, biting her lip.

"Like," Anthony prompted.

Why shouldn't she tell him? He knew so much already. And he'd been there for her in a way almost no one else had. Rae took in a deep breath. "Like my mother," she said in a rush. "She got put away when I was a baby. She died in the hospital a few months later."

Anthony's head jerked back slightly, but his expression stayed the same. He cut a sidelong glance at her. "Do you think she had the same thing you did? Maybe she wasn't really, uh, sick, either."

"I didn't fell you everything about her," Rae admitted. "She wasn't just put in an institution because she was *sick*. It was because—" Rae couldn't say it. She'd never told anyone this part. She tried not to allow herself even to think it. "She did something terrible," she finished. "But they found her unfit to stand trial, so she was put in the hospital."

Please don't ask any more questions, Rae silently begged.

"I don't know what to—wow," Anthony mumbled. "That sucks."

She could hardly believe she'd spewed like that, gotten so close to telling him everything. But riding in the car in the dark, it was like a weird kind of slumber party—where the conversations always got really intimate, confessions of fears and crushes and dreams coming out all over the place.

Rae let out a long sigh. "I guess that didn't really answer your question. The answer is, I don't know if my mom had the fingerprints thing. But I hope she didn't. Because if we're alike in that way, maybe—"

"You're not your mother," Anthony cut in. "My mother and me—we're nothing alike."

"You could be like your father," Rae suggested. She knew he'd wondered about that. He'd never told her, but once she had matched her fingerprints up with his and gotten a wave of Anthony thoughts and feelings.

"Maybe," Anthony answered, keeping his eyes on the road now. "Sometimes I hope I am, just because . . ."

"Because why?" Rae asked, still under the spell of the darkness.

"Because I don't really want to be like either of my stepdads, that's for sure," Anthony answered, his voice edged with iron. "Or any of the various almost-stepdads who've lived with us."

"You don't have to be like your dad to *not* be like them," Rae pointed out.

"Yeah. But . . . I don't know. I'd just like to have the chance to find out. If my old man's like Jesse's, a total waste of space, I'd want to know. Jesse doesn't sit around hoping his dad will call one day or just walk in—" Anthony stopped abruptly.

"I get it," Rae told him. She had an impulse to reach out and touch his hand as he steered, but she didn't. "Knowing the truth about my mom hurts. But it's better than having some fairy princess mother in my head. Probably."

"Probably," Anthony agreed. He pressed down on the gas, and they flew faster into the night.

Chapter 4

"**A**re you sure it's on this street?" Rae asked. She was sincerely hoping Anthony would say no. She'd thought Jesse's neighborhood was kind of run-down, but the houses on his street were palatial compared to these . . . shacks. That was pretty much the only word for them.

"That's what the guy at the gas station said," Anthony answered, inching the car along the narrow street.

"And we should definitely be listening to some loser who pumps gas for a living," Yana said from the backseat. She'd woken up cranky, Rae noticed. Like a little kid.

"We definitely *should,*" Anthony told her. "Those guys always know how to hook you up with stuff."

"If that's true, why didn't they give you an actual *address?*" Yana complained. "I don't know why we need fake IDs, anyway. We can all pass for eighteen."

"You probably can. And I can," Anthony said. "But she—" He jerked his chin toward Rae. "She can't."

"She does have kind of a baby face," Yana agreed.

"Hey," Rae protested. Baby face sounded like code for round, fat chipmunk face. And she had cheekbones. Not amazing ones, like Lea's, but they were there.

Yana leaned over and patted her on the head. "A sweet little baby face," she cooed. "I bet all the prep guys fall all over themselves when you walk by."

"You're forgetting that they all think I'm insane," Rae shot back. Yana smacked her on the shoulder. She always got pissed when Rae used words like *insane* about herself.

"Okay, now, that looks like the home of somebody called the chicken man, don't you think?" Anthony asked.

"Oh my God. I didn't think there would be actual *chickens,*" Rae said. But there were. About six of them crowded together in the tilting coop on the front porch.

"Oh my God. I didn't think there would be, like, actual *chick-ens,*" Yana repeated, doing a decent Rae imitation. She and Anthony cracked up. They were doing that thing—that thing where there are three people and two of them don't know each other, so they bond by making fun of the one they both *do* know.

"I didn't say 'like,'" Rae muttered as Anthony maneuvered the Hyundai into a small spot between two parked cars. He opened his door and climbed out, Yana right behind him. Rae really didn't want to go inside, but she wasn't going to give the two of them something else to laugh about. She jumped out of the car and headed across the weed-choked lawn and up to the porch. The chickens went crazy as Anthony knocked on the door.

"Why would anyone have chickens?" Rae mumbled. "I mean, hasn't he heard of a grocery store?"

"They're for his sacrifices," Yana whispered. "Didn't you hear Anthony say he's a voodoo guy?"

Rae had an impulse to reach over and yank open the door of the coop. No animal deserved to be killed for such a ridiculous reason. *Maybe on the way out,* she thought. After *we get the IDs.*

The door swung open, and her plans to free the chickens evaporated. It was all she could do not to stare at the chicken man. He was tall, definitely over six feet, and so thin, he seemed to be made mostly of bones, bones and the masses of matted hair that fell past his shoulders. "Well, don't just stand there on my porch. Come in and tell me what you want."

Anthony, Yana, and Rae obediently followed him inside. Rae's eyes flicked over the room, jumping from the row of crude dolls—voodoo dolls, she realized—to the jars of murky liquids, to a metal bowl with a small fire burning inside it, a fire that gave off the unmistakable smell of singed hair.

"You looking for gris-gris? Something to protect you from the evil spirits?" the chicken man asked.

"We were looking more for something to protect us from evil bouncers," Anthony said, not seeming at all weirded out by the freaky stuff surrounding them.

"Oh, man. I put on the wig for that?" The chicken man pulled off his matted hair, revealing a dark brown crew cut underneath. "Well, come on in the back." He tossed the wig on a rattan chair with a back so high and wide, it could be a throne, then led the way through the door, which was painted a deep rich red and covered with purple symbols.

When Rae stepped through the door, she felt like she'd entered another universe. Or at least another house. The walls were painted bright white, and the small room was empty except for a long table that had photo equipment in one corner and some kind of machine—Rae figured it was a laminating machine—in the center.

"All right," the chicken man said. "Money first. Fifty bucks a pop."

"I heard it was twenty-five," Anthony answered. Rae's eyes widened. He'd said in the car that he didn't know how much the chicken man charged.

"You sure you didn't hear it was thirty?" the guy challenged.

"Yeah. Maybe that was it." Anthony grinned, they all forked over their money, and the chicken man picked up his camera.

He's slick, Rae thought. *If Marcus were here, he'd have just handed the guy the money without saying a word.* Of course, Marcus wouldn't have even been there in the first place. He'd probably have turned around the second he saw the chickens.

God, why did she keep thinking about Marcus?

"Okay, who's first?" the chicken man asked.

"Anthony, you go," Yana instructed. "Rae and I need to glam up. I want to put some more makeup on that baby face of hers so she'll look a little older."

"Good idea," Anthony said.

Rae felt herself blush. She never wanted to hear the expression *baby face* again. Yeah, she didn't look as sexy as Yana with all her earrings and her tattoo. But she wasn't a chipmunk head, either.

"Is it okay if we use your bathroom?" Yana asked the chicken man.

"Straight through the door," he answered. "Everything in this place is straight through the door. The rooms are all in a row. It's a pain in the butt."

Yana grabbed Rae's hand and tugged her across the room. "We'll be back in a minute," she said. Then she pulled Rae into the bathroom and shut the door behind them. The bathroom didn't have anything too freaky in it—except for the porcelain frog toilet brush holder, but that was more cheesy than freaky.

"Should we change into our other clothes first?" Rae asked. "We could go grab them out of the car."

"Uh-uh." Yana shook her head. "It would look weird if our IDs have the same clothes we're wearing. How often would that happen, right?"

"Right," Rae agreed. She never would have thought of that on her own. Even though she *didn't* have a baby face, she felt like she had kind of a baby brain, at least compared to Yana and Anthony. Yeah, she'd made it through a summer at the funny farm and was doing okay being *gifted,* but when it came to fake IDs and the like . . . clueless.

Yana yanked open her massive purse and studied the contents for a moment. "I think this is the lipstick for you. Baby got mouth. And you should make sure everybody sees it."

"I have put on makeup before, you know," Rae snapped, but she took the lipstick out of Yana's hand, glad her layer of Mush kept her from getting any thoughts. It wasn't cool to peek into someone's head, even if they didn't know she was peeking. At least except when she had to, like to find out if Jesse's dad knew anything about where he was.

"Don't get all bent," Yana said. "I like the makeup you usually wear. It's just kind of quiet for a bar."

"Yeah, which is why I wear it that way for *school*," Rae answered. "You've never seen what I wear when I'm going out."

"Okay, okay," Yana muttered as Rae put on a coat of the dark bruised-cherry-colored lipstick. And she didn't say a word as Rae started making up her eyes using her favorite going-out liner, a silver one that went on all cool and slick and made her eyes look even bluer.

She tried to remember the last time she'd worn the liner, the last time she'd even gone out. It was the party at Robert Mandon's, she realized. Lea had come over to her place first, and they'd gotten ready together. Rae'd wanted to look amazing for Marcus, and she'd tried on so many outfits and so many different makeup combos that Lea had finally threatened to leave without her.

But I guess it worked, Rae thought, using a stick foundation on her forehead, nose, and chin to smooth out her skin tone. That night she and Marcus had gone farther than they ever had before. If they'd been alone—without people banging on the door every few seconds—well, things might have gotten pretty intense.

At least that hadn't happened. If she'd gone for it with Marcus and then he'd dumped her for Dori— tears started to sting Rae's eyes just thinking about it.

"Hey, are you all right?" Yana asked as she finished applying a pair of fake eyelashes studded with little rhinestones.

"Yeah," Rae told her. "Just got a little makeup in my eyes." *No more thinking about Marcus,* she ordered herself.

Yana dug around in her purse again and pulled out a container of glittery powder and another makeup brush. She dipped the brush in the powder and lightly ran it over Rae's curly hair. "Now you have sparkle highlights," she said. "This stuff looks weird in my hair. It doesn't go good on the bleach job." She spread some across her cheeks, giving herself a glow. "You ready?"

Rae nodded, and they headed back into the ID-making room. "Took you long enough," Anthony mumbled. His eyes lingered on her face for a second, and then he quickly glanced away, tinges of red on his cheeks.

"Stand over there in front of that piece of blue

curtain," the chicken man told Rae. As soon as she did, he snapped her picture, then motioned for Yana to take her place. "I'll make you both nineteen. No use pressing your luck. You want to use your own names?"

"Sure," Yana answered. "Then we won't mess up."

"Give me some old ID so I have something to work off of," the chicken man said. Yana handed over her driver's license. Rae gave him an expired gym card. He headed over to the table without another word and started working, his motions sure and economical.

When he handed her and Yana the fake IDs, still warm from being laminated, Rae reminded herself to toss her card before they got back to Atlanta. It wasn't something she ever wanted her dad to see. *He'd* end up in the hospital if he did.

"Don't get in any trouble tonight," the chicken man told them. "No drinking and driving. Your spirits would come after me for sure."

"You don't really believe in that crap, do you?" Yana asked.

The chicken man smiled. "Mostly no, sometimes yes."

"And those chickens in front. You don't really—" Rae began.

"Don't worry, baby," the chicken man interrupted. "Just for show."

Baby again. Rae rolled her eyes.

"We've got to get going," Anthony said. "Thanks for the discount," he told the chicken man.

"Just the regular price, dude," he answered, laughing. He led them back through the freaky room and gave them a half salute as they headed out the door.

"So where exactly is this Hurricanes place?" Yana asked when they were all back in the car.

"I found it on the map. It's not that far. Over on Bourbon Street," Anthony answered, concentrating on extricating the Hyundai from the parking place.

"Come on, Rae. We have to get changed." Yana patted the spot next to her.

In the *car?* Rae almost asked. But she didn't. It would probably just get Yana and Anthony laughing at her again. She wiggled her way into the backseat as Anthony did a Y turn and headed out of the chicken man's neighborhood.

"I borrowed one of your bras, too," Yana told Rae. "With that sheer shirt I borrowed, it's all about the bra."

"That's cool," Rae answered. She pulled her arms inside her T-shirt, then pulled her head inside, too. It was like being in a tiny tent. Then she struggled to get into her sequined halter top without giving anybody in another car—or Anthony—a show. Changing from her jeans to her favorite BCBG black pants was easier since the lower half of her body was pretty much hidden. She jammed on her silver ankle boots, with their skinny high heels, and she was finished.

"Done," Yana said a second later.

"Just in time," Anthony told them. "Hurricanes is right up the street." He inched his way into another barely-there parking spot.

"I love this place," Yana yelled as they crossed the street. She had to yell because there was a different kind of music coming out of every bar, plus some boom boxes on the sidewalk. When they hit the sidewalk, they had to weave through a crowd of people—obvious tourists, college students, suits—watching some kids break dancing. Then almost immediately they had to get through another crowd surrounding a guy who was doing some kind of extreme juggling act with hatchets. Finally they managed to get into the short line leading into Hurricanes.

Rae pulled her ID out of her purse, hesitated, then stuffed it into the front pocket of her pants. She shouldn't have it out, like she was expecting to get carded.

Yana gave her a nudge, and she moved up a step. Then another. And she was in front of the bouncer, a big, buff guy who looked like he should have his own exercise video.

"I need to see some ID," he said. Rae had it out of

her pocket and into his hand in a second. The bouncer flicked his gaze over the ID. Then back up at her. "The chicken man does good work. But there's no way you're nineteen."

Anthony slid into the driver's seat and slammed the door. "Crap," he muttered.

Rae got in the shotgun seat, and Yana took her usual place in back, filling up the car with their girlie smells—hair stuff and makeup, some kind of musky perfume from Yana, and that clean, grapefruit scent that Rae always wore. It still seemed strange that someone would choose to smell like a grapefruit, but he had to admit, on Rae it worked. Like it warmed up when it combined with her skin and got kind of . . . sexy.

"Sorry, guys," Rae mumbled.

"It's not your fault," Anthony said, staring straight ahead at the car parked in front of them. It was too weird looking at Rae in that top, which, whether she knew it or not, was designed to get a guy to stare at her breasts. With her back bare, it was totally obvious she couldn't be wearing a bra, and once you got that info, well . . . that was it.

"So what do we do?" Rae asked.

Anthony looked across the street at Hurricanes, which meant looking past Rae. Except his eyes kept getting snagged. And not just on that sparkly top and what was under it. On her lips. On her hair. Her hair drove him crazy—there was so much of it, and it was so curly, that he was always wondering what it would feel like to burrow his hands into it.

Knock it off, he ordered himself. How could he sit there obsessing over a girl's hair when Jesse was missing?

"Maybe there's a window in the guys' bathroom I could go through," Anthony said, forcing his mind back to his most immediate problem. Then he shook his head. "But that wouldn't really help."

"The two of us could probably get in with our IDs," Yana told him.

"But we need Rae," he answered without thinking. He shot a glance at Yana in the rearview mirror. She didn't look like she thought it was strange that they needed Rae to ask a bartender a few questions.

They sat in silence for a long moment, then Yana broke it. "I think that bouncer liked me," she said. "I bet I can get us in."

"What, you think you're just going to smile at him and he'll fall on his knees and say yes to anything you want?" Anthony asked.

"Pretty much," Yana said. "Stay here. I'll wave to you when it's okay." And she was out of the car before he or Rae could say another word.

Anthony watched her strut across the street. He

had to admit she was pretty good guy bait. "It's still weird that you two are friends," he said, talking without thinking again. *Okay, here's the order—use brain, then open mouth,* he told himself.

"What are you talking about? Yana's great," Rae protested.

"Yeah," Anthony agreed.

"Yeah, but what?" Rae pressed.

Why couldn't she be the kind of girl who let stuff drop? "It's just that you're pretty different," he answered.

"Different how?" Rae asked.

There were the obvious ways—like how they dressed. But the big difference was that even though Yana joked around a lot, Anthony got the feeling that she was hard inside. Kind of like him. And Rae—Rae could come off hard sometimes. But it was like she'd had to learn to be that way to get through the hospital. It was more of a shell—not her center.

"Different how?" Rae repeated, a twinge of that very hardness in her tone. Defense mode.

He didn't think she'd especially like the whole soft-versus-hard thing. "Uh, you know. You're all prep school, and she—"

"That's such bull," Rae interrupted. "Why are you and Yana so hung up on the private school thing? The people who go to my school are just . . . people."

Yeah, rich people. Smart people, Anthony thought.

"Have you ever even been inside a public—" he began. Then he caught sight of Yana waving frantically from across the street. It looked like she'd been waving for a while. "Come on," he told Rae. "I guess we're getting in after all."

When they got back to Hurricanes, the bouncer waved them in with a bored expression on his face. "I found out from my new best friend that Luke's on a break right now," Yana said as they stepped inside. "He'll be back in about fifteen," she added, her voice rising to compete with the music. "He has red hair and a Ren and Stimpy tattoo."

"Great," Anthony said, impressed. Although he wasn't at all impressed by Hurricanes itself. There were chairs and tables attached to the ceiling, which was okay since they were going for the whole hurricane deal. But the place was not even approaching clean, which was taking the theme a little too far. The walls seemed almost oil coated. And the crowd . . . the only thing he could say about the crowd was that it looked like it belonged in the bar. Which wasn't exactly good.

"You know what this means? We have time to dance!" Yana cried. She grabbed Rae by one wrist and Anthony by the other and pulled them deep onto the dance floor.

Anthony was not a dancing kind of guy. Any other

physical thing—football, swimming, running, base-ball, basketball, even gymnastics—he was fine with. But not dancing. It made him feel like a dork. Which was only compounded by the dorkishness he was already experiencing now that Rae and Yana were both towering over him in their friggin' high heels. Usually he and Rae were almost exactly the same height, but now he felt like he should be singing, "We Welcome You to Munchkin Land."

"You two go ahead," he muttered. But Yana didn't let go of him. She just started shimmying, still hold-ing on to his wrist. And how much dorkier would he look trying to pull away from a hot girl? The answer—much, much dorkier. So he started shuffling his feet a little, trying to blend.

He noticed that he was getting some stares. And not what-a-dork stares. More like what-a-lucky-guy stares. He started getting into the dancing a little more, his hips loosening up. *Yeah, go ahead and look,* he thought. *Look at me here with two total babes.* Babes who were way too tall, but babes.

A skeevy-looking guy, kind of oil coated himself, who had to be pushing forty—hard—danced his way up to them. "You've got more there than you can han-dle," he told Anthony. "Why don't I take this one off your hands?" He reached for Rae.

In one second Anthony had his body positioned in

front of Rae's. "I don't think so," he said. And the guy assumed the stance, the stance that said that he and Anthony weren't going to get out of this without some blood spilled on the floor.

Which Anthony had no problem with. Taking this guy out wouldn't be a problem. And it would be fun.

It would also get him booted from the bar.

Now you've got it, he told himself. *Use brain before mouth—or fists.*

"Look, man," he said. The guy seemed like someone who'd say "man," and Anthony figured it would be good to sound like the same kind of guy. "You don't just walk up to a beautiful girl and say you'll take her off my hands like you're doing me a favor. It's insulting."

Rae stepped out from behind him. "Totally insulting. You need to work on your approach."

Anthony wished she'd stayed put, but at least she was following his lead. And Yana was staying out of it. Watching the whole thing as if it was one of those reality TV shows that she'd flipped on for entertainment.

The guy ran his fingers through his thinning blond hair. "Okay, you're right," he said, sounding almost weepy. Anthony realized he was way drunker than he'd seemed at first. "Would you like to dance with me?" he asked Rae.

"No, thanks," she answered. "But that was better."

"You know what would be really great," Anthony jumped in, hoping he wasn't pushing things too far. "You should go up and ask the band to play a love song. If you do, you might get her in the mood to say yes."

The guy smiled. "Thanks, man," he said. And he turned around and headed toward the band. Rae and Anthony looked at each other for a moment, and then they both started to laugh.

"Pretty smooth, Anthony," Yana said.

"It should give us time to ask our questions and get out of here. Let's head for the bar. Luke should be back any minute," Anthony answered.

"Hey, Yana, why don't you see if you can get any more info from your bud the bouncer?" Rae asked. "Find out if Luke's taken any time off lately, been late more, that kind of stuff. Maybe talk to a couple of the waitresses, too."

"Good idea," Anthony said. It *was* a good idea. It was also a good way to keep Yana out of the way while Rae did her fingerprint thing. Not that Yana would know that's what she was doing, but clearly Rae didn't want her to see it, anyway.

"I'm on it," Yana answered. She started dancing her way through the crowd. Anthony put his hand on Rae's back, and they started pushing their way off the dance floor and over to the bar.

"Nuclear shot?" the woman bartender called over

the heads of the people pushed up against the bar. "A dollar apiece for the next minute and a half."

"Okay, we'll take two," Anthony answered. Who knew how much a beer would cost in a place like this. He was just looking for something to hold so he could hang by the bar, and something that cost a buck sounded good to him.

The bartender handed over two neon green test tubes. Anthony passed one to Rae, who took a tiny sip. "Remember, we're not going to actually mention Jesse," Anthony told her. "That will either piss him off or shut him up."

"Right," Rae answered. "Looks like it's show time." She nodded toward a red-haired guy squeezing his way behind the other bartender.

Anthony plunged through the crowd at the bar, Rae right behind him, wanting to reach Luke before he got a ton of orders shouted at him. "We're looking for my little brother," Anthony called, managing to catch Luke's eye. "He disappeared about a week ago. Last seen around here."

"He's thirteen. Red hair. Blue eyes. Talks a lot," Rae added. She grabbed a cocktail napkin off the bar and wiped off her fingers, getting ready to work. "We thought maybe you'd seen him around, like when you were coming here."

Anthony watched Luke's face, searching for any

kind of reaction. But he didn't catch a flicker of fear or guilt or anything. "He's really into skateboards. He might have had one with him."

"Sorry," Luke answered, concocting some kind of fruit drink. "You've seen what it's like outside. Madness. Tons of people all the time. If I saw the kid, I don't remember."

Rae leaned over the bar and grabbed the drink as soon as Luke was done. "This looks awesome. I have to have it. You can make another one, can't you?" She slapped down some money, and Luke shrugged, then started mixing another drink.

Anthony turned to Rae as she ran her fingers over the entire glass. She leaned close so she could speak right into his ear. "Nothing that says he's lying so far."

Anthony nodded. She'd just confirmed what his gut had told him while he watched Luke's face.

"You know any places a kid might end up? Shelters or squats or anything?" Anthony asked, not willing to give up just yet.

"We've got to find him. Jerry—that's his name, Jerry—he's not so, you know, mature for his age." Rae's voice caught. Anthony glanced over at her and saw that her eyes actually had tears in them. "I'm just afraid . . ." She shook her head. "Sorry. I—do you have a Kleenex?" she asked Luke.

"Best I can do," Luke answered, handing her

another napkin. "I wish I could help you out. But I'm not a kid kind of person. I don't know where he'd be."

"Thanks," Rae said. She pulled Anthony away from the bar. "That time I got him wondering how old Jesse was the last time he saw him. He was actually kind of sad." Rae squeezed Anthony's arm. "Luke doesn't have him."

Where are you, Jesse? Anthony thought, feeling like his heart had turned into an ice-making machine that was pumping frozen little pellets through his body. *Where the hell are you?*

Chapter 5

"**A**h, the beautiful Gretna Motel Six," Yana said as she flopped down on the closest of the two double beds. Rae sat down next to her and pulled off her silver boots.

/ Anthony handled / hope the place is /

"I don't care where we are as long as there's a shower," she answered. "That bar left me feeling like I've been rolling around in grease."

"But we found out what we needed," Anthony reminded her. He closed the door, locked it, put on the chain, then stretched out on the other bed and closed his eyes.

He looked wiped out—wiped out and worried—with shadows under his eyes and tight jaw muscles.

"We're going to find Jesse," Rae promised.

"When we're driving home tomorrow, we'll make a plan."

Anthony didn't respond. She opened her mouth to say something else but stopped herself. He wasn't the kind of guy who let himself be reassured by empty words.

"I don't know about you guys, but I'm starving," Yana announced. "I'm going to check out the vending machines."

"I'll go, too." Anthony sat up with a groan. "But I should call home first."

Rae glanced at the cheapo clock radio. "It's pretty late. Almost midnight. Won't you wake people up?" She'd checked in with her dad when Anthony was hitting up the gas station guys for info on where to get IDs.

"My mom and stepdad are probably still out partying," he answered. "And if they're out, no way are the kids in bed." He grabbed the receiver, studied the little stick-on dialing directions on the phone, then punched in some numbers.

"Zack, you're getting paid to baby-sit, right?" Anthony asked, without even bothering to say hello first. "So why do I hear Carl crying and Anna and Danny screaming their heads off?"

"He sounds like a dad," Yana whispered to Rae. They exchanged grins. Anthony ignored them, listening to the whiny voice Rae could hear coming through the phone.

"They should all be asleep, anyway, but since they're not, tell Danny that he picked the last show, so Anna gets to pick the next one, and they only get to watch one and that's it," Anthony said. "And did you make Carl take his antibiotics?"

The whiny voice said something, and Anthony shook his head. "It doesn't matter if his ear doesn't hurt anymore. He has to keep taking the pills until they're gone."

"But Dad," Yana mouthed to Rae, and they both got an attack of the giggles. Yana grabbed a pillow off the bed and pressed it lightly against Rae's face. But they both kept laughing.

"Nothing," Anthony said, responding to a question from the whiny voice. "Just a couple of idiots."

"A couple of idiots," Rae repeated, her voice muffled by the pillow. She pulled it away from Yana and tossed it at Anthony's head. He let the pillow bounce off without trying to catch it. "Can't you just do it?" he asked. The whiny voice whined some more. "Fine," Anthony said impatiently. "Put him on." He slid over to the other side of the bed and faced the far wall.

Clearly he didn't want Rae and Yana to hear him. Yana put her fingers to her lips, and she and Rae leaned forward, determined to catch every word.

"Okay, Carl. But just one time, then you have to go to bed," Anthony said. Then he started to sing. *Sing.* "Froggy went a courtin'; he did ride, uh-huh."

"How sweet is that?" Rae said softly, the desire to giggle drained out of her.

"It's kind of pathetic," Yana answered, and her voice had an edge to it. *She's not kidding,* Rae realized. How could Yana think it was pathetic that tough guy Anthony Fascinelli was willing to sing to his little brother? Especially in front of other people. God, it was turning Rae into butter inside.

She and Yana listened in silence as Anthony finished up the song. "Now, bed," he ordered. "I'll see you tomorrow," he added, then quickly hung up.

"Vending machines?" Yana asked immediately.

Rae glanced around for her purse but didn't see it. "Can I borrow the keys, Anthony? I left my purse in the car."

He pulled them out of his pocket, started to toss them to her, then hesitated, gave them a fast rub on his shirt, and handed them to her with the tips of his fingers. Rae shot a look at Yana, wondering what she'd thought of that little performance, but she was rooting around for change in the bottom of her bag.

"Get me something, and I'll pay you back," Rae said. She jerked her boots back on, ignoring the blurry repeats of her thoughts, then strode over to the door, unfastened the chain, and opened the lock, touching the metal as little as she could. *I hope he doesn't expect me to turn the doorknob with my teeth,* she thought. She couldn't help feeling annoyed, even though she knew she wouldn't want anybody picking up random thoughts from *her.* She reminded herself to put on some more Mush when she got back upstairs.

Rae took another glance at Yana, who was still digging for change, then used the heel of her hand to polish the knob before she opened the door and headed out into the dingy hallway. She pressed the down button of the elevator with her knuckle, and the elevator door slid open immediately. Rae stepped in and knuckled the button for the first floor. When the elevator door opened again, Rae hurried out, made a right by the little pool, and headed to the parking lot.

It felt a lot creepier without Yana and Anthony with her, and she got a prickly feeling in the back of her neck. Like someone was watching her. *Yeah, because muggers, they always stake out the Motel Six parking lots,* she told herself sarcastically. *They know anyone who stays in a Six has got tons of cash.*

But it wasn't really muggers she was worried about. This parking lot was like a movie set for a murder. A fast knife between the ribs or a—

Stop, she ordered herself. *Yes, someone tried to*

kill you. And yes, they could try again. But no one knows you're here. You're safer in this grungy parking lot than you are at home in bed, where everyone expects you to be.

She half convinced herself, but she was still relieved when she got to the car and unlocked it. She gave the door handle a quick polish, then scrambled inside. *See, Anthony? Even when you're not around, I'm not trying to go poking in your head.*

Okay, now purse. All she had to do was snag it, and she could get back upstairs. But it wasn't on her seat. It wasn't in the backseat, either. Rae scanned the floor. Nope.

She leaned forward, her forehead pressed against the dashboard, and started groping around under the front passenger seat. Her fingers brushed up against something smooth—

/MORON/FRIGGIN' BLUEBIRD/DOES RAE/

—and she pulled it free. It was the English workbook, the one she'd thought belonged to Anthony's little sister. But the thoughts she'd gotten off it were all Anthony flavored. And they were so full of self-loathing that it made her stomach cramp.

Rae flipped open the workbook to a page that had already been filled out. There were spots where the answer had been written and erased so many times that the paper had a hole worn through it. And the name printed at the top of the page was Anthony Fascinelli.

No wonder he'd freaked the day she'd found the workbook in the glove compartment. Anthony had told her he was in a slow learner class, but clearly he didn't want her to know how much trouble he was really having, how behind he was.

Gently she pushed the workbook back under the seat, another blast of self-hatred and anger ripping through her. It was like when he thought about himself, all he thought was stupid, stupid, stupid. "He has no idea what a great guy he really is," Rae muttered.

She gave the workbook another push. She didn't want Anthony to get himself in knots wondering if someone had seen it. "Don't worry, Anthony. I'm very good at keeping secrets."

Anthony studied the row of chips in the vending machine. *Cool Ranch,* he decided, feeding the machine three quarters, then hitting the E3 button.

"So, sounds like you have a big family," Yana said as her diet Dr Pepper shot into the tray of the soda machine with a thunk. "How many brothers and sisters?"

"Three brothers—Danny, Carl, and Zack—and a sister, Anna," Anthony answered. "Zack is step, and Anna, Danny, and Carl are half." He slid some more quarters in the slot and punched the button for a two pack of chocolate chip cookies. He could split it with Rae.

"All younger?" Yana asked.

"Yep. The oldest one, Zack, he's fifteen. Then there's Danny. He's eleven. Then Anna, nine, and Carl, who's three." Anthony counted up the change he had left. "How about your family?"

"Just me and my dad," Yana answered.

"Like Rae." Anthony decided on another two pack of cookies—all chocolate this time.

Yana snorted. "Yeah, like Rae," she agreed, oozing sarcasm. "Have you ever met Rae's dad?"

"Huh-uh," Anthony said, turning toward her. "Why? What's the deal?"

"It's just that Rae's his whole life," Yana answered. "You should have seen him when she was in the hospital. He was a wreck. For a while I thought he was going to need to check in himself."

She's jealous, Anthony thought. He knew the feeling. Sometimes he'd see a family at the movies together, and—he didn't let himself finish the thought. "I'm sure your dad would have been the same way if you were in the hospital," he told Yana, jamming some more change into the machine, then jabbing the closest button.

"Oh, thanks," Yana said, still in full-on sarcastic mode. "You're right. I never, ever thought of that." Another soda shot into the tray, hitting the other one. "You've never even met my dad," she answered.

"Whatever," Anthony muttered. She was right. He should have just kept his mouth shut.

Yana scooped up the sodas, and Anthony gathered up all the crap he'd bought, then they headed back to the room. "My dad . . ." Yana hesitated. "It can be cool. I mean, I get to do pretty much whatever I want." She gave a harsh laugh. "Rae's dad probably still checks her homework and everything. He's a college professor. I'm sure he expects her to go to some great school."

Anthony managed to unlock the door without dropping anything. "I guess pretty much everyone who goes to prep school is supposed to go to a great college. That's the point, right?" Like he'd know.

"Like I'd know," Yana answered. "But yeah, I guess." She whipped the thin plaid bedspread off the closest bed and spread it out on the floor. "Picnic," she said, pointing to it.

Anthony sat down on the spread and dropped his load of vending machine junk. Yana put down the sodas, then headed into the bathroom. She returned a moment later with three glasses, their little paper tops still on them. "Rae probably doesn't drink directly from the can," Yana said as she took a seat across from Anthony. "Too, too uncouth," she added, going for a snotty upper-crust accent.

"Yeah," Anthony agreed, even though he'd seen Rae drink out of a can and knew Yana had, too.

"Do you think they teach that stuff in her school? Etiquette stuff?" Yana asked. She didn't wait for him to answer. "I bet they teach them how to walk. When I picked Rae up from school, everyone I saw walked the same way, like they had a stick up their butt."

Anthony laughed. Rae did stand up pretty straight all the time. "You couldn't pay me to go there," he answered. As if he could ever get in. But even if he could, there was no way.

"Me either," Yana answered.

There was a knock on the door. "It's me," Rae called.

Anthony felt a little spurt of guilt for talking about her behind her back. But it wasn't like they were saying anything so awful. She *was* a prep school girl.

Yana flopped onto her back and moaned. "I can't eat another bite."

"Shhh. You'll wake up Anthony," Rae whispered.

"Oh, no! We'll be in big trouble if we wake up Dad," Yana teased.

Rae opened her mouth to respond, but a burp came out instead.

Yana shook her head. "What was that?"

"A burp. Sorry," Rae answered.

"Do they teach you to burp like that in prep school? All dainty?" Yana asked.

Rae snatched up the last soda—the Mush protecting her from getting any thoughts—popped the top, and drained it, ignoring the little stream running down the side of her chin. Then she gave the biggest, longest, loudest burp she could. *Take that, public school reverse snob,* she thought.

"That's disgusting," Yana told her.

"Disgusting for a prep school girl?" Rae demanded.

"No, just disgusting disgusting," Yana answered.

Rae smiled. "Good." She stretched out on her side and propped her head on her hand, then checked to make sure that Anthony was still sleeping. "So what do you think of our Anthony?" she asked.

"I was wrong when I said I knew the type," Yana answered. "The type I was thinking of would never have sung that frog song."

"I still say it was sweet," Rae told her. She unbuttoned her pants. That last soda had left her feeling ready to burst, and the waistband was digging into her stomach.

"If you like sweet," Yana answered. She picked up a piece of cookie and licked it, then dropped it back on the bedspread.

"You don't like sweet?" Rae could see Yana with a nice guy. She was so supportive and sensitive, really there for people she cared about. Why shouldn't she get some of that back?

Yana shrugged.

"You're not getting away with that," Rae told her. "I want some details. What was the last guy you went out with like?"

"I don't really go out that much," Yana answered.

Rae frowned in confusion. Yana seemed like the type who'd go out all the time, with tons of guys waiting in line for their chance.

Yana picked the piece of cookie back up and popped it into her mouth. "Actually, if you want to know the truth, I don't go out at all. I go out and dance and stuff," she added quickly. "But I've never done the one guy/one girl thing."

"Maybe you're better off," Rae said, thinking about Marcus. "You won't get your heart smashed that way."

"I wouldn't mind trying it," Yana admitted. "I just . . . I don't know. Guys go for girls more like you."

"What do you mean—like me?" Rae asked.

"Longer hair, no tattoos. You know," Yana answered.

"Come on. I bet there are tons of guys out there who think you're totally hot," Rae protested. "If no one's approaching, maybe it's because you don't act like you want anyone to. Guys like to have some idea that they're not going to get shot down if they come up to you."

"Maybe," Yana admitted.

"Not maybe. Definitely," Rae insisted. "Because we both know it's not about hair and tattoos. I've seen girls with no hair and a zillion tattoos with guys. And not repulsive guys, either." She smoothed the corner of the plaid bedspread, then smiled at Yana. "So, is there anyone in particular you are so sure wouldn't want to go out with you?"

Yana didn't answer. But she blushed. Actually blushed.

Rae sat up. "There is! So who is he?"

"Just a guy," Yana muttered.

"And have you given this just-a-guy any signals?" Rae pressed. "Have you ever even smiled at him?"

"What if he thinks I'm a loser?" Yana asked. "I don't want to be the pathetic girl who goes after some guy who's out of her league."

"Okay, first, if you use the word *loser* about yourself again, I'm going to slap you," Rae threatened. "And second, what guy could possibly be out of your league? You're awesome."

Yana laughed. "Yeah. All males shall bow down and worship me," she said. But Rae could tell she still hadn't convinced Yana even to say hi to this guy, whoever he was. She had some work to do tonight.

For once we're talking about her problems and not mine, Rae thought. It meant that they were real friends. Equals. Yana wasn't just doing her good deed of the day by hanging out with Rae.

Rae closed her eyes for a moment, letting the feeling sink in. As worried as she was about Jesse, it was still cool to feel like she and Yana were getting closer. Hopefully soon they'd have Jesse back, and then Rae could concentrate on convincing Yana to go after everything she deserved to have.

Chapter 6

"**W**here should I drop you?" Anthony asked as he pulled out of Yana's driveway the next evening.

"It's okay to take me home," Rae answered. "My dad meets up with a couple of people in his department every third Sunday to—dork alert—play bridge. So he won't be around."

Anthony nodded. The car felt a lot quieter without Yana. Smaller, too. Which was weird. It should have felt bigger with one less person. Except without Yana's musky perfume, all he could smell was Rae's grapefruit scent. Without Yana's yammering, he could hear each breath Rae took. He could almost feel the heat coming off her skin.

Why had she worn that friggin' halter top last

night? It was like seeing her in it had flipped a switch, and he couldn't quite get back to seeing her in that pre-halter-top way, even though she was back in one of her regular button-down prepster shirts with a bra underneath. A lacy bra. He could kind of see the pattern, just faintly—

I've got one word for you, Anthony told himself. *Cardinal.* No, make that two words. *Cardinal* and *Bluebird.* He and Rae weren't even the same species. Or maybe all birds were the same species. But whatever. Cardinals and Bluebirds didn't hang together. They hung with their own kind.

"We're going to find him," Rae said, giving his arm a fast squeeze.

It took Anthony a second to understand what she meant, then guilt swept through him, strong as battery acid. Rae thought he was all knotted up about Jesse, and Anthony'd been thinking about *her.* What a guy. What a freakin' jerk.

"I'll pick you up after school tomorrow, and we'll hit some of his usual places," Anthony answered. "You can do your fingerprint thing on anybody we find that knows him or has even seen someone who looks like him."

If he was going to find Jesse, he needed to focus on Jesse. Nothing else. *No one* else.

Usual places. He needed a list. Little Five Points,

definitely—the skateboard shop and the comic book store, and the place that sold all the loose candy. Jesse loved the atomic fireballs there. Jesse's school. The 7-Eleven, although Jesse didn't hang there very much without Anthony.

"Any ideas on where to—" Rae began.

"I'm thinking," Anthony interrupted, without looking at her.

"Well, don't let me disturb you," Rae muttered.

He pretended he hadn't heard her. He had to keep focused. Where else? He thought Jesse played b-ball at the park over on Magnolia. He didn't go to the mall that much, but he might have ended up over there. What was the name of that kid with the fully loaded computer? He and Jesse played some kind of on-line game over there. Was he even from Jesse's school?

"I know you're *thinking* and everything, but if you're still taking me home, you should have turned left back there," Rae told him.

Anthony made a U at the next light, without bothering to comment. His silence clearly made her somewhat pissed at him, and he kind of thought that was a good thing—focuswise. He split his attention between the road and coming up with more places to look for Jesse. When he pulled into Rae's driveway, she jumped out like her butt was on fire. "So pick me up after school," she said, then slammed the door and strode toward the house without looking back.

He had this impulse to run after her, and, he didn't know, apologize or something. But it wasn't like he'd actually done anything to her. He couldn't help it if she was so freakin' sensitive. Anthony backed out of the driveway and headed for home.

When he walked in the front door, he wished he was still in New Orleans—even in the chicken man's freaky front room. His gaze flicked from Carl, who was eating what looked like Lucky Charms off the living-room carpet, to Anna, who was watching the Powerpuff Girls at an eardrum-piercing level while trying to keep the remote away from Danny, who was yelling almost as loud as the TV. Zack, the so-called baby-sitter, was nowhere to be seen. Neither was his mother.

Anthony strode over to the TV and shut it off, which briefly stopped the fight between Anna and Danny because they both started yelling at him. Zack wandered in from the kitchen, holding a box of Snackwells. "I scored lunch," he announced.

"Lunch," Anthony repeated. "Lunch. That's lunch?"

"Luuunnch. What part of it didn't you understand?" Zack shot back as he ripped open the box.

Anthony didn't answer. He just headed into the

kitchen. All the cabinet doors were hanging open, and he was starting to see how Snackwells could seem like lunch. It wasn't like they could eat a box of baking soda or some vanilla. He slammed the closest cupboard shut. What was his mom thinking? Yeah, she was always sort of a flake, but she usually managed to remember to go grocery shopping.

This was *so* not his problem. But what was he supposed to do? "Everybody in the car," he shouted. "McDonald's run. If you don't know what you want by the time we get there, you're not getting anything." He didn't plan on making a many-houred excursion out of the trip. And Tom and his mother were paying him back.

"Can I get large fries?" Danny asked.

"Yes, you can get large fries," Anthony answered, imitating his little brother's shrill voice. He heard the front door bang shut, and by the time he reached the living room, it had been cleared out. He checked the front pocket of his jeans to make sure he had the keys, then headed out to the car.

When they got to McDonald's, Anthony automatically did a quick scan of the place. It was possible that Jesse could be there. But he wasn't, although Anthony spotted Brian Salerno.

"Yo, fat 'n' smelly," Salerno called from across the room. Zack snickered at Anthony's grade school nickname but only for a second—only until Anthony gave him a fast knuckle to the back of the neck.

"Hey," Anthony answered. He didn't bother to sound at all friendly, but of course Salerno came on over, anyway, joining Anthony's group and cutting in front of the couple who'd gotten into line behind them. Salerno had just never figured out that he and Anthony weren't, never had been, and never would be buds.

"So you ready for English tomorrow?" Salerno asked.

School. Why was the idiot Salerno bringing up school? It was the last thing Anthony wanted to think about. Like he didn't have enough to stress about without imagining sitting in his Bluebird English class with all the other morons, trying to read one sentence out loud without screwing up.

The most important thing is getting Jesse back, he told himself. Screw English. Screw everything else until he and Rae got Jesse back. Yeah, Rae wasn't a quitter—even if she was a little pissed off—and neither was he. They wouldn't give up on Jesse, no matter how long it took.

Rae dutifully copied the definition for *simile* in her notebook—picking up some staticky thoughts, all hers, from the pencil—even though she already knew exactly what a simile was. How could she not, living with her dad? She glanced up and found her English teacher, Mr. Jesperson, looking at her. He did that a lot. Clearly he hadn't gotten over the idea that she needed a special "friend," someone to help her adjust to being back at school. *Forget it, Mr. J.,* she thought, returning her gaze to her notebook. *You and I aren't going to be doing the inspiring-after-school-special thing.*

"Okay, all teachers are scum. Is that a simile or a metaphor?" Mr. Jesperson asked.

Anthony's exercise book flashed into Rae's mind. Nothing about similes or metaphors in there. Just stuff like when you should use an apostrophe. She could still almost feel those spots that had been nearly erased through. Feel the self-disgust that oozed through Anthony, like if he couldn't read that well, he was a total loser in every way.

The bell rang, jerking Rae out of her thoughts. She jammed her notebook into her backpack, grabbed her purse, and rushed out. She wanted to get out of there fast in case Mr. Jesperson decided he wanted a little heart-to-heart before lunch.

Rae's steps slowed as she started down the hall-way. She hesitated, then veered to the left, heading away from the cafeteria and toward the library. She wanted to look up some info about learning disorders.

Maybe there was something Anthony could do, something his teacher wasn't trying, that would make the English thing easier for him.

And while you're doing this good deed, you can skip going to the caf, which you hate. What a saint. But she didn't turn around. She pushed open the door and stepped into the quiet of the library, then headed to the closest computer monitor and typed in *dyslexia*.

Maybe dyslexia wasn't what Anthony had, but it was the reading problem she'd always heard about, and Rae figured it was a good place to start. She jotted the call numbers of a couple of books on the cover of her notebook and tracked them down without a problem, then settled herself in one of the little cubbies at the last table in the back.

"Okay, *The Rewards of Dyslexia*," she mumbled. She flipped open the book and started to read the intro. Basically it said that people with dyslexia thought in images, which let them think a lot faster than people who thought in words. Which was a good thing—there were scientists and artists who probably couldn't have done the stuff they'd done if they hadn't been dyslexic.

Rae wondered what Anthony would think if she told him that. Would he actually get that having a different kind of thought process didn't mean he was a moron?

She kept reading. It turned out that even though

people with dyslexia could be really smart, they had trouble reading because if a word didn't call up a picture in their mind—even a really easy word like *the*— it was hard for them to understand it. Pretty soon if there were too many words without images attached, a dyslexic got brain overload so bad, they could even start feeling dizzy or disoriented.

Which would probably totally piss Anthony off. He liked to be in control. And who could blame him? Rae was sort of a control freak herself. Just knowing that Jesse was out there somewhere and they couldn't find him . . .

Rae shuddered. *This is about Anthony,* she reminded herself. Someone she *could* help. She scanned the table of contents and found a chapter that gave some exercises that could help dyslexics with words that didn't bring up images. *Maybe Anthony and I could do some of these together,* Rae thought. She flipped to the chapter and started taking notes. *Make that a very big maybe.* It wasn't like Anthony would be happy that Rae wanted to help him. He didn't like to be helped. They were alike in that way, too. Plus there was the little problem that Rae wasn't supposed to know how badly Anthony needed help.

Rae kept taking notes. She'd deal with how to get Anthony to try the exercises later. For now she'd just get them down.

Someone took the seat in the cubby next to her, but she didn't even glance up.

"Hey, Rae," a low voice said.

Rae scooted back her chair, already knowing who she'd find sitting next to her. Yep, it was Marcus freakin' Salkow, looking amazing as always. She didn't say anything, just raised one eyebrow, waiting.

"Hey," Marcus said again. Then he started doing his teeth-clicking thing.

"Hey," Rae muttered. She started to get up from her chair, but Marcus reached out and blocked her with one arm.

"I keep thinking about, you know, the other day in the hall," he admitted. He leaned down and tightened the knot on his sneaker, even though it didn't need tightening.

Rae had this wild impulse to reach out and rest her hand on his silky blond hair. She twisted her hands together until her nails pressed into her skin. "The day when you were a butt head, you mean?" Rae asked.

"Yeah," Marcus agreed softly, not bothering to defend himself.

Why couldn't he have gotten ticked and left? She really didn't want to listen to him stumble his way through some totally lame excuse again. Especially not while she was getting these freakish urges to touch him.

Marcus clicked his teeth. He glanced around nervously, as if he wasn't sure exactly where to look. Clearly he was still having trouble looking directly at her.

"Remember the ancient Egypt section?" he asked, nodding toward a row of books a few feet away.

Rae's lips got hot and tingly. Did she remember that section? Oh, yeah. Another hot spot started up in her stomach. How could she forget? Back in that row of books wasn't the first place Marcus had kissed her, but they'd had a few make-out sessions back there that were . . . molten.

She swiped her hand across her mouth, lipstick smearing across her palm. "Are you asking me to go hook up with you back there?" Rae asked. "Is that the deal? You think I'm so pathetic that I'll be happy to jump all over you like it's some kind of favor?"

"That's not—" Marcus began to protest.

"I guess you haven't gotten Dori trained yet." God, he was just like Jeff, sniffing around her because he thought she'd be desperate since no one at school would want to be with her. As if she wouldn't rather be alone. Rae stood up and grabbed her notebook, the dyslexia books, her backpack, and her purse, letting her old thoughts wash through her.

"No," Marcus snapped. "You stay. I'm gone. All I was trying to do was explain—" He slung his backpack over his shoulder. "Forget about it." He strode away.

Rae stood there, holding all her junk in her arms. Had she totally misinterpreted him? Was he just asking her if she remembered the ancient Egypt section because it was a nice memory for him and he thought it would be for her, too—even now?

She took a step forward. She could still catch him. Then she dropped everything back on the table. Whatever his deal was, it was better to let him go. She had much more important things—and people— to worry about.

Chapter 7

I wish she'd hurry the hell up, Anthony thought. He didn't like even sitting in the parking lot of Rae's school. Everyone who passed him had to know he didn't belong here. Even if he wasn't sitting in a freakin' Hyundai, they'd know. But with the Hyundai it was like taking out an advertisement. He leaned back his head and closed his eyes so at least he wouldn't have to see the people watching him.

A few moments later the passenger door swung open. Anthony opened his eyes and watched Rae slide into the seat and slam the door. "Ready to roll?" she asked. She didn't seem at all pissed off today. Rae clearly wasn't one of those girls who made a guy pay for weeks for one mistake. But then, he and Rae weren't boyfriend and girlfriend, and that was usually when—

He stopped himself and pulled out of the parking lot.

"Yana called me this morning before school," Rae said. "She wanted to say good luck. Actually, she wanted to come and help us, but she's doing some project for school with a completely militant partner."

"We don't really need her," Anthony answered. Although it wouldn't have been a bad thing. Rae's grapefruit perfume or lotion or whatever was already filling up the car. And it was . . . distracting. *Cardinal,* he reminded himself. He turned on the radio, cranked it, and drove to Little Five Points faster than he usually drove. He pulled into the parking lot of the strip mall where the comic book store was, then he and Rae headed inside.

The vampire-pale guy behind the counter didn't look up from the comic he was reading until they were standing right in front of him. "You know Jesse Beven, right?" Anthony asked as Rae headed down the closest aisle, running her fingers across a long row of comics.

"Have a Silver Surfer on hold for him," the guy answered. "Not for much longer. Supposed to pick it up two days ago."

He shot a look down at his comic. Anthony reached out and covered it with his hand. "When's the last time he was in?"

The guy let out an exasperated sigh. "A week.

About." He used two fingers to try and get Anthony's hand off the comic. Anthony kept his hand where it was. "Sweat damages the pages," the guy informed him.

Anthony realized his palms *were* sweating. The back of his neck, too. And his underarms—a sweat factory. *It's 'cause you don't think this is going to work,* a little voice in the back of his head whispered. *It's 'cause you don't think you're ever going to see Jesse again.*

Shut up, he ordered himself as he pulled his hand off the comic. "If he comes by, would you tell him Anthony's looking for him?" he asked. *Right. Like he's going to just come strolling in,* the little voice commented. Anthony tried to ignore it.

"Uh-huh," the guy muttered, already back to his reading.

"I want to pay for the comic—for Jesse," Rae said as she wandered up to the counter. She slid a twenty in front of the guy. When he gave her the change, Anthony saw that she made sure to touch his fingertips. Anthony studied her expression, but it didn't seem like she was learning anything.

"Nothing," she said as soon as they got back outside. "I mean, nothing useful. I did get a thought of Jesse's off one of the comics I touched, but it was an old one. He was thinking about being late to group."

"It's only our first stop," Anthony answered.

"Let's leave the car parked and walk around. There are a bunch of places near here Jesse hits pretty often." *A bunch of places where no one's going to have seen anything,* the doom-spewing part of his brain commented as Anthony led the way across the parking lot. He wished he could just switch off that part of his brain. Every time it yapped, his body pumped out more sweat. His T-shirt was plastered to his back, and his hair was slicked to his scalp. He pressed his arms close to his sides, hoping he didn't reek.

"I keep thinking about Jesse's mom," Rae said as they headed past the strip mall and down the next block. "She's got to be going crazy. I wish we could at least tell her that Jesse's father doesn't have him."

"It would make her even more nuts to know that we went and talked to Luke," Anthony answered. "She'd never feel safe in Atlanta again. She wouldn't be sure he didn't get some info out of us that he could use to track her down."

"Yeah," Rae agreed, stepping over a buckled section of sidewalk. Anthony caught one of his hands reaching out to steady her and jammed both hands in his pockets. The girl could take care of herself.

A couple of kids around Jesse's age came speeding around the corner, one on a scooter, the other two on skateboards. "You guys know Jesse Beven?" he called out. One of the kids came to a stop in front of him; the other two swerved around him and Rae and kept on going.

"Is he okay?" The kid used his toe to flip his board on end, then picked it up.

The sweat coating his body turned to ice. "What do you mean, is he okay?" Anthony demanded.

The kid flicked one of the wheels on his board. "I heard that some guy pulled him into a van the other day."

It's not going to do any good to tear his head off, Anthony told himself. *Stay calm. Stay freaking calm.* "Tell me everything," he said. Rae moved closer to him. She grabbed a handful of the back of his T-shirt and held on tight.

"Chris, the dude at the skateboard place said he saw Jesse get shoved into a van by this big guy with a purple Mohawk. It was last week sometime. I wasn't sure if Chris was messing with me. He makes stuff up sometimes. But I haven't seen Jess around." The kid gave the wheel another flick. "So is he okay?"

Anthony didn't answer. He just ran, stumbling over the uneven sidewalk, Rae right behind him, still holding on to his shirt. At the end of the block he took a right, then cut across the street and into the skate-board shop. "I need to talk to Chris," he announced the second he and Rae were inside.

A tall, thin guy dressed all in spandex headed toward them. "I'm Chris."

"We're looking for Jesse Beven," Rae answered before Anthony could. She gave the cloth of his T-shirt a twist. "We think you're the last person who saw him."

"Yeah," Chris answered. "I saw this guy with a Mohawk pull him into a van."

A kid who'd been studying one of the boards turned toward them. "No way. That lady pulled him out of here, remember?"

"What lady?" Anthony demanded, turning toward the kid.

"I figured it was his mom," the kid answered. "She didn't look happy. Jesse's probably just grounded or something."

"A lady?" Rae repeated.

"What did she look like?" Anthony asked, his words running over hers.

"Short. Kind of chubby. Red hair, like Jesse's," the kid answered. "His mom, I figured. Am I right?"

"Don't listen to him. I'm telling you a guy with a purple Mohawk—" Chris began.

"You're both losing it," the girl behind the counter said. "I saw the whole thing from the window. Jesse headed out, and then he fainted or something. An ambulance came and picked him up."

"Deirdre, you've been watching way, way too many soaps," Chris told her. "You're losing your grip on reality."

"Yeah," the kid agreed. "His mom came in and dragged him out. He probably had been slacking on taking out the garbage or he took money from her purse or some bull like that."

Deirdre shook her head. "I saw what I saw. And since I'm not chemically enhanced most of the time, I think you guys should listen to me," she told Rae and Anthony.

What the hell is going on? Anthony wondered. They'd gotten three stories in three minutes. And Anthony's instinctive lie detector wasn't going off. He couldn't pick up any signs that he and Rae were being fed a line.

Rae reached out and shook Chris's hand. For an instant she got that blank, not-Rae look, then she pulled her hand away. "Thanks for your help," she said. "If Jesse comes by, tell him Rae and Anthony were trying to find him."

She shook Deirdre's hand next, then the kid's, then she led the way out of the place. "What's the deal?" Anthony asked, hoping she'd gotten something that would take them straight to Jesse but almost sure she hadn't.

*   *   *

"The deal is that all three of them were telling the truth," Rae answered. She rubbed her hands together, trying to feel like herself again. All these not-her thoughts and feelings were still swirling around inside her.

"What's that supposed to mean?" Anthony ran his hands through his hair, and Rae saw the deep circles of sweat staining the T-shirt under his arms.

"I don't know what it means," Rae admitted. "But when I touched their fingers, I didn't pick up anything that said any of them was lying."

"That's bull!" Anthony exploded.

"I agree. But—" Rae gave a helpless shrug. "That's what I got."

Anthony looked like he'd really love to punch something. Rae totally understood. But they had to stay focused. "Look, obviously something happened right around here. Let's just talk to some more people." She scanned the street. "We could start with that homeless lady. She's probably in the neighborhood a lot."

"Okay. Let's go." He spit out the words, and Rae could see his struggle to keep himself under control in the tight muscles of his neck and shoulders. Even the muscles of his arms looked clenched.

I think I'll do the talking, Rae decided as they approached the woman, who sat on a faded piece of carpet in front of a vintage clothing store that had gone under. "Excuse me, my little brother is missing. He comes around here a lot, and I thought you might have seen him."

The woman didn't answer, but she seemed to be listening, so Rae hurried on. "He's thirteen. Red hair. Blue eyes."

"On a skateboard a lot," Anthony added. He pulled out his wallet and slid out a photo of Jesse. The woman nodded when she saw it.

"A couple of skinheads snatched him," the woman said. "Shoved him in the back of a station wagon with the windows painted black."

"Can you describe them more? Or the car?" Anthony asked.

The woman's forehead creased as she thought for a minute. "Not really. You know—skinheads."

Anthony shot Rae a look, and she knew what he wanted her to do. She pulled a ten-dollar bill out of her purse. The woman looked like she could use it. "Thanks for your help," Rae said, pressing the money into the woman's hand, making sure their fingertips touched.

The instant they did, Rae's mind was no longer her own. It was filled with the homeless woman's thoughts, layers and layers of them. Scraps of memory. Fragments of childhood fears. Pieces of dreams. Her stomach cramped with hunger. She felt a dull headache just behind her eyes. Her lips felt the sweetness of a first kiss. A ball of pure pain filled her chest, the pain of a lost child.

Her instinct was to try and block the thoughts and feelings. It was too much. Too personal. Too overwhelming. Too *fast*. She was hit by so much information, so much emotion simultaneously that she felt like she was being pounded into the cement. *Let it come,* Rae told herself. *Let it come.*

A thought about the red-haired boy, about Jesse, joined the cacophony. Skinheads. Station wagon. The thoughts were clean and clear. Rae released the woman's fingers. She'd told them all she knew.

"I hope you find him," the woman answered.

"Thanks," Rae said. She and Anthony headed down the block. "She was telling the truth, just like the others," she told him when they were out of the woman's earshot.

"They can't all be telling the truth," Anthony burst out.

"I got the thoughts really clear, clearer than any of the other thoughts," Rae said.

"Is that normal?" Anthony asked.

Rae took a deep breath. "I don't know what's normal yet," she replied, shaking her head. "Especially in the fingertip-to-fingertip thing. I mean, normal kind of went bye-bye for me a while ago."

Anthony nodded. "I guess we should ask around at the Chick Filet up there." He gave a disgusted snort. "Like it will help."

"You never know," Rae answered, although she had the same bad feeling Anthony did. The Jesse situation had gotten stranger and scarier. It felt a lot more out of control than it had yesterday. "I just need a couple of minutes before I touch fingertips again. My head is feeling kind of gooey. I'm getting the headache everyone else had—right behind the eyes."

"What do you mean, everyone else?" Anthony asked as they headed into the fast-food place.

"All the people I touched to get thoughts from had a headache," Rae answered. "Or maybe I gave them a headache by doing it, which would make more sense than four random people having a headache right in the same spot."

"When you did it to me the other time, it didn't give me a headache," Anthony told her.

"Weird. But you know my motto—Weird 'R' Me," Rae replied.

"I guess." He paused. "Not that you're weird," he added quickly. "That *it's* weird." He got in the shortest line. "Since we're taking a break, I'm getting some waffle fries."

"Me, too. And a massive Coke," Rae said. "Then as soon as we've scarfed, we'll get back to work."

She tried to make herself sound confident and determined. But when she glanced at Anthony, she didn't think he'd even noticed the effort. He'd clearly gotten so caught up in his own thoughts that she could be a hundred miles away.

Maybe while we're eating, I could talk to him about the dyslexia book, she thought. It wasn't exactly the perfect time. But they needed more info before they could come up with a better plan to find Jesse, so . . . she might as well bring it up, right? Her stomach tightened as she tried to figure out exactly what she could say, how to bring it up without being totally offensive.

She still hadn't come up with anything good by the time they'd gotten their food and found a table. Probably because there wasn't any good method. But that didn't mean she shouldn't do it. The info she'd gotten could change Anthony's whole life, the way it had some of the people's in the book.

"Want ketchup?" Anthony asked, holding up some of the little packets.

"I'm not a ketchup girl," Rae answered. "I like them plain—so I can really taste all the grease and salt." She popped a waffle fry into her mouth and kept right on talking. Which was gross, but she was nervous. "I had this baby-sitter once who used to put vinegar on her fries. Is that nasty or what? She was from Canada."

"Huh," Anthony grunted.

Whatever that little babble fest was, it was *not* any kind of intro into talking about a learning disorder. Rae took a swallow of her Coke—

I so going to quit!

—then another one, then she tried again. "I was reading this interesting book the other day. It was about dyslexia."

Not too smooth. But acceptable. At least she thought so until she saw Anthony's face. It was blank, a total mask of a face. Whatever he was thinking or feeling, he wasn't going to let her in. And since he wasn't saying anything, he definitely wasn't going to open the door she'd knocked on.

But too bad for him if he didn't want to hear it. This was too important to just drop.

"Remember when you figured out where I was getting all my psycho not-me thoughts?" she asked.

"Yeah," Anthony said. She was surprised he could get a word out past his mask face. "So?"

"It totally changed my life. Really," Rae said. "And, um . . ." This was the tricky part. "Um, there's something I want to do for you. A thing like what you did for me."

"Like what?" Anthony asked, with exactly zero amount of interest.

"Like in that book I was telling you about, it gave

some exercises for people"—Rae lowered her voice—"people who have trouble reading. I thought maybe you and I could—"

"I never told you I had any problem reading," Anthony interrupted, his voice as low as hers but rough with anger.

"You said you were in a slow learners class, remember?" Rae asked, forcing herself to look him in the eye.

"I never said anything about reading," Anthony repeated. "You got it off my workbook, didn't you?" he demanded. "You touched it when you were going through the glove box, before I got it away."

It would be easier just to say yes. Easier, but not the way to go. The one thing she and Anthony had always been able to do was be honest with each other. "I didn't touch it that day," she answered. "But when we were in the motel and I went down to get my purse out of the car . . . it was an accident. I hadn't put the Mush back on. I was feeling around under the seat and—"

"And now you want to do your good deed and play teacher," Anthony spat out, his eyes flashing with anger. "All you prep school girls do volunteering and crap. Looks good on your college applications."

"That's not—" Rae began to protest.

Anthony shoved away his fries. "These things are cold. They're making me want to hurl." He stood up. "If you want to talk to more people with me, fine. But that's it. One word out of you about anything but Jesse and you can find your own way home."

"Fine," Rae snapped. "I was trying to do you a favor, but fine. I'll stay and help you out. For Jesse."

* * *

I've been watching you, Rae. And I don't think you're enjoying the game I arranged for us to play together. You looked so confused when you tried to find out the truth about what happened to Jesse. It didn't even occur to you that I'd put thoughts into the heads of the "witnesses" you found.

Innocent Rae. If you knew that your mother had the same ability, the ability to make people think what she wanted them to think, you might have a clue. But you only know what Daddy's told you. I thought that maybe you'd inherited your mother's ability. But I was wrong. If you had, you wouldn't have looked so pitiful and puzzled. And you would have implanted a thought of your own, a thought that would have negated mine. Then you would have realized that none of the people really saw what happened to your Jesse, that it was all just smoke.

So we'll continue our game. Our game of What Power Does Rae Have? And once I know what you can do, then I'll decide what kind of revenge I'll enjoy the most. I'm looking forward to that.

Chapter 8

Anthony checked the clock, always a big mistake at school. English still had another twenty minutes to go. And there were hours and hours before gym, the only class that didn't make him want to puke. Wonderful.

He noticed a few people flipping the page in the ancient *People* magazine they were reading—Ms. Goyer, the teacher, had decided that they needed more interesting reading material—so he flipped the page, too. For a couple of minutes he actually listened to Phil Amagast read aloud about the latest Hollywood supercouple breakup. That was about as much as he could take because not only did Amagast read incredibly slowly, like all the Bluebirds, he had allergies or something and he kept sucking snot back into his nose. Plus was Anthony actually supposed to care that some big-shot actor and his plastic wife had split up a while ago? The magazines were so old, everyone already knew what had happened, anyway.

Amagast paused to pull in what sounded like a truckload of snot, then he went on—word, wet sniffle, word, um, um, word, wipe nose on sleeve, word, uh, um, word. . . .

A craving came over Anthony, like hunger, like thirst, like the need to piss first thing in the morning. He wanted a doobie. He could almost taste it, the thick smoke in his lungs, the world becoming just a little bit nicer.

He glanced at the clock again. Only three minutes had passed. *Get a bathroom pass,* he told himself. Mike or Gregg might be in the can. Or at least somebody who could give him a toke. He didn't need a lot. Just enough to take the edge off . . . so blood wouldn't come gushing out of his ears after his brain imploded, which was sort of what it felt like was happening. Anthony started to raise his hand, then lowered it and gripped the side of his desk until his fingers ached. If he let himself get a little buzz to get through the day today, then he'd be back to getting high all the time. And that was not the best way of getting out of this friggin' place for good. He wanted to graduate, and he was barely making it through his Bluebird classes pot free.

In that book Rae was talking about, was there really a way that—

Stop, he told himself. *Remember fourth grade— getting on the moron bus, going to that place where all everyone wanted to do was help little Tony?* Freaks couldn't even get his name right. And the crap they made him do—it just made him feel even stupider.

And then there was the seventh grade. Mr. Leary. *Discipline means a disciplined mind.* He couldn't breathe in that guy's room without getting the dictionary treatment—standing in front of the class, arms out, with a massive dictionary balanced on each palm until his muscles quivered, until he had to drop the books no matter what Leary said. Friggin' Leary.

Anthony's skin started to get hot. Hot and itchy. He could feel each spot where a hair connected to his skin. If he didn't get out of here—

Jesse. Think about Jesse, Anthony ordered himself. What could the deal be? He and Rae had talked to a bunch more people in Little Five Points yesterday. Some of them had seen Jesse. But all of them had a different story about what happened, just like the first few people they'd talked to. What could that mean? Some kind of drugs in one of the coffee bars in the area? A blast from an alien mind-altering laser beam after Jesse was abducted? Hypnosis? Mass hysteria?

Anthony knew his theories were getting way out of control. But the whole situation was insane. *There has to be an explanation,* he told himself. But he had no freaking idea what. And why? Because he was so friggin' stupid. How was he supposed to get Jesse back when he could hardly read two words in a row and basic math problems made his head turn inside out?

Cut it out, Anthony ordered himself. He hated it when he started getting all snively and self-pitying. *Okay. Jesse.* An image of the kid flashed into his mind, followed almost immediately by an image of Rae, her face pale and scared.

Somebody tries to kill Rae, he thought. *Then Jesse disappears.* Could there possibly be a connection? What did Rae and Jesse have in common? They both were in group therapy at Oakvale. What else? They'd both helped clear Anthony of setting the pipe bomb. Which meant they'd both helped put David Wyngard away. So, some kind of revenge thing? But with all those people involved? It made no sense. It—

"Anthony, do you remember?" Ms. Goyer asked, bringing him out of his thoughts. "Without looking at the magazine, can you tell me what the name of their youngest son is?"

"Uh, Booger?" Anthony answered, because he had no idea. It was a totally lame joke, but the

Bluebirds laughed anyway. They were probably all bored out of their skulls.

"No," Goyer answered, with her usual poor-learning-disabled-child smile. "Want to try again? I'll give you a hint. It has nothing to do with bodily functions."

"I know," Andi McGee volunteered. She lived to volunteer answers, even though she got them wrong as much as the rest of them did.

"Let's let Anthony try first," Goyer answered.

Then—holy freakin' miracle—the bell rang. Anthony was out of the trailer the class was held in and down the aluminum steps before anyone. His steps slowed as he headed toward his math class. *Just three more until gym,* he told himself.

He gave himself the new score after every class. *Just history and two more until gym. Just drafting and one more until gym. Just freaking tutorial with freaking head-too-big-for-his-spindly-little-body Anderson. Now gym.*

Anthony made it from the tutorial to the locker room in less than thirty seconds. The instant he was inside, he pulled in a deep breath. God, he loved the smell of old sweat and feet and mildew. It was almost as good as weed. It actually gave him a minor buzz.

He headed over to his locker, used the key to open it—he hated combination locks—and changed into his sweats. Then he strolled into the gym with five minutes to spare. He decided to run the bleachers until everybody else showed up.

A couple of stretches and he was off, running straight up to the top of the bleachers, then back down, across the basketball court, and right up to the top of the opposite bleachers. Back down. Back across. Back up. Back down. Back across. All the hours of bull he'd had to endure that day faded, then disappeared. His body became his whole world.

"Fascinelli," he heard Coach Meyer shout. Anthony spun halfway toward the voice, taking the bleachers sideways. A football came spiraling toward him. Anthony caught it without breaking stride. When he heard Meyer on the bleachers behind him, Anthony swerved right, then left, faked another swerve right—which totally fooled Meyer—and angled up to the top stair, then plunged back down, feet pummeling the wood. When he reached the floor, he turned back and did a little victory dance with the football.

"Not bad," Meyer said. But he grinned, and Anthony could tell he was at least a little impressed. "If you'd just apply yourself—"

Anthony's buzz disappeared. He knew what was coming.

"To your classes the way you do to sports, your

GPA would be off the charts. More than high enough to qualify you for a spot on the team," Meyer continued.

"Uh-huh," Anthony muttered. Like it was just laziness keeping him in the moron brigade.

"I need a strong running back on the team," Meyer continued. "You're my first choice. I could talk to your teachers. If they can tell me you're progressing—"

"I'm not a joiner," Anthony interrupted, noticing that about half the class had shown up in the gym and was listening to the exchange.

"What the hell is that supposed to mean?" Meyer demanded.

Anthony tossed him the ball, then turned away.

"I don't understand you, Fascinelli," the coach muttered.

You and Rae both, Anthony thought. If there was a way he could change, didn't they friggin' think he'd have done it by now?

Rae headed straight into Oakvale. Usually she waited for Anthony, but she had the feeling he still wasn't done giving her attitude for daring to try to help him, and she didn't see any reason she had to put up with that. She was going to help him with Jesse, but that was it. Unless he managed to pull his head out of his butt.

She hesitated in the main hall, then decided to go

upstairs. She had to pee, and the downstairs bathroom gave her the creeps. She knew it was ridiculous. She knew that the odds of someone planting a second pipe bomb in there were billions to one. But she'd still rather not use it.

Not that it's totally creepy free up here, she thought. The second floor was deserted. But at the same time Rae kept getting the prickly-back-of-the-neck feeling that somebody was watching her, through a crack in one of the doors or on some kind of hidden camera. It was a feeling she got a lot lately. Not just at Oakvale. Everywhere.

"Get a grip. You're imagining it," she muttered as she stepped into the bathroom, using her elbow to open the door. She peed, washed her hands, did minor makeup repairs, brushed her hair, put on a little more perfume, just basically stalled, ignoring the old thoughts touching her stuff brought into her mind, then headed back down to the group therapy room with about four seconds to spare. The only seat that was empty was next to Anthony. Figured. Rae took it. Anthony grunted something that might have been a greeting. Rae resisted the urge to grunt back. "Hey," she mumbled, lacing her hands together to eliminate any accidental touching of stuff. She was glad that Ms. Abramson didn't waste any time getting started.

"Hopes and dreams," Ms. Abramson said, beginning to pace around the inside of the circle of metal chairs. "Nothing is more important. Without hopes and dreams, there are no goals. No accomplishments. No new visions in the world. No heroes. No stars. Today I want you to pair up and help each other discover what your hopes and dreams are. Ask each other questions. Really listen to what is said. Then ask some more. When you're done, each of you will tell the group about what your partners aspire to do and become."

Rae turned away from Anthony toward Shawn Miller. But Shawn had already turned toward Kim Feldon. Reluctantly Rae turned back to face Anthony, just as he was reluctantly turning back to face her.

"So. You first. Dreams," Rae said quickly. She planned on controlling this little session.

"Don't have any," Anthony answered. "What about you?"

"Don't have any, either," Rae shot back. They stared at each other for a long moment. "I don't buy it, anyway," Rae finally said, breaking the silence. "You have to have something you want to do."

"*I* have to have something, but *you* don't." Anthony shook his head. "How does that make any sense?"

"Look, it's different for me, okay?" Rae answered. "I just want to be normal. Not have people think I'm a freak anymore."

Anthony raised one eyebrow. "You're lying," he announced. "You don't want to be normal. You want things to be the way they used to be, before, you know." He wiggled his fingers at her. "And I'm one hundred percent positive you weren't happy just being normal then. I've seen girls like you."

"Girls like me," Rae repeated. She didn't ask him what that meant. She knew it was just going to piss her off.

"Yeah, girls like you," Anthony went on, uninvited. "Got to have the perfect clothes. The perfect boyfriend. The perfect everything. Got to be the girl that all the other girls want to be. Which isn't being normal. Normal's not nearly good enough for a girl like you. If you thought you were normal—at least before the whole meltdown thing—you probably would have wanted to slit your wrists."

Nailed. So much for me being in control. A few questions and Anthony already had gotten her eyes stinging with unshed tears. Rae drew in a long, slow breath. Then she tried to answer calmly. "Maybe I was like that. Maybe that is what I wanted." Actually, there was no maybe about it. From the time she'd hit junior high, Rae had been completely focused on making it into the school elite.

"But even if I wanted that now, it's a ridiculous thing to have as a dream. It's never going to happen.

Not unless I develop the ability to turn back time." She was talking to herself as much as Anthony. Laying out the logic, trying to make herself believe it deep down where she still kind of didn't.

"Abramson didn't say the hopes and dreams had to be possible," Anthony answered.

"Only pathetic losers have dreams that don't have any chance of coming true," Rae told him. She might be a freak. She might be a social pariah. But she wasn't going to be a loser.

"So you're saying there's nothing else you want. If you can't be Little Miss Popular Prep School Girl, you're just going to lie down and die because that's the best thing that could happen to you in life," Anthony said.

"Look, you said you didn't have any dreams at all, so it's not like you're—" Rae began.

"We're talking about you right now," Anthony interrupted. "We're talking about what a shallow, spoiled little rich prep school—"

"I know your dream," Rae said triumphantly. "*You* want to be a rich prep school guy. That's why you're always ragging on me. It's because you want it, and you can't have it." His expression barely changed, but his eyes narrowed the tiniest bit, and she thought the rate of his breathing picked up a little. *Direct hit,* she thought. But the burst of triumph faded. It didn't make her feel that much better that Anthony had something he wanted but couldn't have.

"The only reason I'd want to go to your school is that they have the best football team in the state," Anthony answered. "That's it."

"Would you say that's a dream of yours?" Rae answered. "To play on the Sanderson Prep team?" She hoped Anthony could tell it was an attitude-free question. She really wanted to know the answer.

Anthony played with the slit ripped in the knee of his jeans. "Maybe," he finally admitted, a flush climbing up his throat.

"I can see you doing that. I mean, you're not—" Rae stopped herself from finishing the sentence. She hoped Anthony wouldn't realize she'd been about to say, "You're not that tall." "You've definitely got the build, all muscley and everything," she said, starting over. "I bet you're good. And it's not like everyone who goes to Sanderson is rich. They have scholarships."

"Are you forgetting who you're talking to?" Anthony burst out. He yanked on the slit in his jeans, and the denim ripped further. "Or is there some special scholarship for morons that I don't know about?"

Rae reached out and pulled his hand away from the hole in his jeans, careful to keep her fingertips away from his. "Did you listen to anything I said yesterday?" She kept her voice so low, there wasn't a chance anyone else could hear it. "Being dyslexic, which you definitely could be, doesn't mean you're a moron. It just means your brain works differently than most people's. Like I told you, people with dyslexia have made all these advances in tons of areas because they *do* think differently." She tightened her grip on his hand. "The book had a bunch of different techniques to help dyslexics adapt. Why won't you at least let me tell you about them? Why won't you let me help you?"

Anthony eased his hand out of hers. "Okay," he muttered.

"Okay?" Rae repeated. She could hardly believe she'd heard him say the word.

He nodded, not quite looking at her. "Okay."

Chapter 9

"**S**o, none of you have seen Jesse in at least a week?" Anthony asked, searching the faces of the kids who had been playing basketball in the park.

Rae gave him a nudge, then jerked her chin toward a kid who was way too involved in positioning his water bottle in his backpack. Looking at him gave her a tingling sensation all down her spine. He clearly didn't want to talk to them. And maybe whatever he was keeping secret could lead them to Jesse.

Anthony tossed the ball he'd been holding to the closest boy, then strode over to the kid kneeling next to his backpack. Rae followed right behind him.

"I guess you heard we're trying to find Jesse Beven," Anthony said.

"Haven't seen him," the kid muttered, fiddling with the zipper on his backpack. It was obvious he hoped if he just kept working the zipper that she and Anthony would go away.

"Let me help you with that." Rae knelt down and jerked the zipper closed.

/can't tell/tattoo/come kill me/

The fear that came with the thoughts made Rae gasp. Yeah, this kid had information. But he wasn't going to give it up, at least not willingly.

"Okay, well, thanks for answering the question," Rae said. She stuck out her hand. For a second she didn't think the kid was going to take it, but then he gave it a hard, fast shake.

It was enough. Rae got her fingertips into position and used her free hand to keep the connection. She was sucked up into a tornado of thoughts and feelings. An old fear of the two strange lights that appeared on his bedroom wall every night. Embarrassment over some stupid nickname his friends had given him. The secret fact that he liked to pretend he was Harry Potter even though he was way too old.

Jesse, Rae thought. She needed anything he knew about Jesse, and time was running out. "Tattoo." She forced the word out, even though it was hard to speak during the fingertip-to-fingertip contact, and she tightened her grip on the kid's hand.

New thoughts exploded in her brain. A dark-haired man with the tattoo of a scorpion on his hand, grabbing Jesse. The man seeing the kid watching. Telling him to keep his mouth shut or the man would be coming after him next. The kid running until he felt like his lungs would burst.

The kid jerked his hand away from Rae's and leaped to his feet. "I've gotta go," he told them as he rushed off. Then he paused and looked over his shoulder. "Good luck finding Jesse." He bolted before either Rae or Anthony could answer.

"I didn't get a lot of details," Rae told Anthony as they headed out of the park. "But that kid was the real deal. I'm sure of it. I didn't think about it before, but those other people I touched when we were asking about Jesse—their thoughts didn't have emotions attached to them. The kid's did. He saw Jesse get snatched, and he's terrified the guy will come after him if he talks about it."

"Did you get any thoughts about the guy? What he looked like?" Anthony asked. He sounded ready to tear the guy's head off.

"The kid didn't have a great memory of his face. He had dark hair. And a tattoo of a scorpion on his hand," Rae answered.

"A scorpion," Anthony repeated. "I feel like I've seen that tattoo. But I can't remember where. I've got that itchy feeling in my head, you know? But it's not coming."

"Maybe if we touched fingertips, I could find the memory," Rae suggested. "But if it's not something you're able to access, I'm not sure how easy—"

"No, you're right. It wouldn't work. If I just stop trying to think of it, it will pop into my head," Anthony said quickly.

He doesn't want to let me in, Rae realized.

"Now I just have to figure out how to think of something else. Because right now all I can think about is Jesse." Anthony rubbed his forehead with the heels of his hands, as if that would help his brain work the way he wanted it to.

"Well, um, I know one other thing you could think about," Rae answered. She cut a glance at him, sure he wasn't going to want to hear what she had to say. "You said you'd be up for trying out some stuff from that book after we hit the park. It's at my house. Would you want to come by for a while? Maybe you'll think of where you've seen the tattoo while we work."

Anthony'd been praying that she'd forgotten about the whole reading thing. Which was pretty delusional because it hadn't been that long since that hopes-and-dreams group therapy exercise. "Okay," he muttered. What else could he say? That he had changed his mind? That he was a total wuss?

"So, I was thinking," he said as they started walking back to the car. "Maybe this stuff with Jesse could have something to do with you."

"What?" Rae exclaimed, her blue eyes widening. She sounded like he'd just accused her of snatching Jesse herself.

"All these people with all these different thoughts in their heads about Jesse," he explained, kicking at the gravel on the path as they walked. "That's pretty weird. And right after someone hired David to set that pipe bomb to ki—to, you know." He cringed, realizing Rae probably didn't need to be reminded about the attempt on her life.

"Kids disappear all the time," Rae answered. She tucked her hands into the opposite sleeves of her sweater as if she was suddenly cold. "It's not so weird. There are a lot of sickos out there."

"That's not the part I meant," he argued. "All those freakin' stories. That's *X-Files* weird. And so is the whole thing with you. The fingerprint thing. Some mystery person out to kill you." Anthony gave a helpless shrug. "Two bizarre things happen in less than a month. It would almost make more sense if they were connected somehow." They reached the sidewalk, then headed down to the car and got in in silence.

"I guess you could be right," Rae admitted. She

fastened her seat belt, and Anthony pulled out into traffic. "But unfortunately, even if you're right, it's not going to help us any. We're as clueless about who went after me as we are about what actually happened to Jesse."

"How are you doing, anyway? With knowing someone is . . ."

"Is probably looking for another chance to kill me?" Rae finished for him.

Anthony nodded, feeling like a moron for not asking more often. Rae wasn't the kind of girl who'd blab on and on about how scared she was. She could be half out of her mind with fear and never bother saying anything to him about it.

"I'm, you know, as well as can be expected," Rae answered. "Except, and this is probably total paranoia talking, a lot of the time I feel like someone is watching me, following me, even."

Anthony's eyes automatically went to the rearview mirror. He saw cars back there, but on this street that was normal. "Have you seen anything?"

He caught Rae doing a rearview mirror check, too. "No. Like I said, it's just a feeling, an eyeballs-on-my-back kind of thing."

All Anthony wanted was to have whoever was after Rae and whoever had snatched Jesse in front of him. He would pummel them until his hands bled and love every second of it. If he could just remember where he'd seen that scorpion tattoo—

"Let me tell you some of what the book said. That way we can get down to work as soon as we get to my house," Rae suggested, pulling him out of his thoughts.

Her house. They were getting way too close to her house. The lawns were getting bigger. The houses were getting bigger, too. Bigger and cleaner looking. Like someone spent all day buffing up every inch with a toothbrush.

"You know what? I think we've got more important stuff to spend time on," Anthony said. "After Jesse's back and after we get whoever's after you put away, then we can—"

"Forget it, Fascinelli," Rae interrupted. "You're not weaseling out of this."

She meant it. That was clear as freakin' glass. Sweat started popping out all over his body. He could hardly read. He could hardly do a simple math problem. But when it came to sweat—he was A-plus all the way.

Anthony turned onto Rae's street, then pulled into her driveway next to the Chevette already sitting there. Great. Her dad was home. And he was some kind of college professor or something. He was going to take one look at Anthony and realize—

"I know. I feel the same way about the Chevette," Rae said, obviously misreading the pained look on his face. "But my dad thinks it's cool. He specializes in Arthurian stuff, so he doesn't have the greatest grip on reality."

Arthurian stuff. Anthony had no idea what that was. He hadn't even met the guy, and already Rae's father was making him feel stupid.

Rae gave the door handle a quick rub with her sleeve—she hadn't put her waxy stuff back on yet—then got out of the car. Anthony got out, too—what choice was there?—and followed her into the house.

"Are you hungry or thirsty or anything?" Rae asked.

"No," Anthony answered quickly.

"Then let's just go back to my room," Rae said, starting down the hall, which had been painted with fluffy clouds. "Dad," she called over her shoulder. "I'm home. And I brought one of my friends from group."

"That's nice," a male voice called back.

"He's relieved that anyone will even come over," Rae whispered. "Other than you, Yana's the only person who has since The Incident." Rae opened one of the doors and ushered him into her room. It was . . . *sophisticated.* That was the word that came—slowly— into Anthony's mind. The walls had been painted to look like green and black marble, and there was a black leather chair in front of the black desk. Total Cardinal room. Just standing in it ramped up the sweat production.

"So, um, sit down and let's get started," Rae said. Anthony glanced at the black leather chair. If he sat in that thing, he was afraid he'd leave a wet streak across the back. But it was the only chair in the room. Anthony cautiously sat down on the edge of the bed, which felt somehow not right.

Rae grabbed a binder off her desk and a magazine off her bedside table, then she sat down next to Anthony. He'd been thinking she'd take the chair, but now he'd have to contend with the grapefruit smell of hers on top of everything else.

"Okay, I want you to read a page of one of the articles in here out loud." She passed the magazine over to him. "Sorry it's *Glamour.* I meant to buy something more manly, but I spaced."

"Whatever," Anthony mumbled. The choice of the magazine was way low on the list of his problems right now. He flipped past the pages and pages of glossy ads, trying not to look too closely at the babes, especially the ones in their underwear. Not that he had to worry about that *other* problem right now. He stopped on the horoscope page, figuring it was as good as anything.

He opened his mouth, then closed it. He couldn't do this. Couldn't. Even if he wanted to—which he didn't—he couldn't. There was no way he would even be able to force out a sound. It was like even his teeth were sweating now.

"It's just me," Rae said, her voice all gentle and understanding.

Just her. Yeah, like that made it easier. She'd seen his workbook. She'd gotten some of his thoughts. But that wasn't the same as actually hearing him attempt to read in his completely pathetic way.

He shot a glance over at her. She was waiting. And knowing Rae, she'd just keep on waiting and waiting and waiting. She was as stubborn as . . . as stubborn as he was.

He stared at the first word in the first paragraph. "Libra," he said, getting an image of a scale. He moved his eyes to the next word. His finger itched to underline it because that helped him focus, but he kept both hands wrapped around the magazine. "Don't"—he got an image of one of those circles with a slash through it—"bet"—a picture of a pile of poker chips flashed into his head. Then he hesitated. He knew the next word was an easy one. It was only two freakin' letters long. *Focus,* he told himself. *Focus.* "On," he said. Out of the corner of his eye he caught sight of Rae making a note in her binder.

Great. He really needed a permanent record of his humiliation. Anthony swallowed. Or tried to. His throat felt about as wide as a piece of wire. Then he moved on to the next word. Crap. Another little one that everyone in the entire world would know with no problem. Everyone except him. He moved his finger over until it was positioned under the word. He didn't care if it made him look stupid. Not being able to come up with the word at all would make him seem a lot stupider.

"An," he managed to get out. He looked at the next word. An image of a blond in a thong filled his head—"easy." A picture of a clock replaced the blond—"time."

He had to stop and think again. Another one of those freakin' baby words. And he didn't know what it was. He felt like a giant hand had just clamped down on his head, pressing through the bones of his skull, squeezing his gray matter.

"Screw it." Anthony thrust the magazine back at Rae and leaped to his feet. With two long strides he was at the door. "We shouldn't be wasting time with this, anyway," he said, turning to face her. "Maybe the tattoo parlors in town keep records of who gets what kind of tattoos."

"It's worth a shot," Rae answered. "We can work on the reading more later." She stood up and took one step toward him.

"Frank," Anthony burst out.

"What?" Rae asked.

"Frank. That's the name of the guy with the scorpion tattoo on his hand. I met him at a keg party I went to with my friend Gregg," Anthony explained.

"Just Frank. No last name?" Rae said.

"Gregg will know how to find him. Can I use your phone?" He didn't wait for her to answer. He rushed over to her bedside table, snatched up the sleek black phone, and punched in Gregg's number. He let out a low curse when an answering machine picked up. "Gregg, it's Fascinelli. I need to ask you something right away. Call me at—" He looked at Rae. She told him her number, and he repeated it into the phone. "First thing, Gregg, all right?" Anthony hung up, hoping Gregg wouldn't be too high to focus on the message.

"So, I guess we don't have to hit the tattoo parlors," Rae said. She sat back down on the bed and picked up her notebook.

"Yeah, but I can't concentrate on anything else now. I don't know how you can, either. With Jesse missing and everything," Anthony said.

"Don't you want to know what the words you had trouble with have in common?" Rae asked, ignoring him.

"They're all freakin' baby words," Anthony answered, flopping down next to her.

"They're all words that don't have images associated with them," Rae countered. "They're all words the book said a lot of people with dyslexia would have trouble with."

Anthony looked over at her, but he didn't say anything. He was afraid of what would come out if he tried.

"Just stick with it for ten more minutes. Less than that if Gregg calls first," Rae urged. "We'll take one word that was a problem for you—" She flipped open the magazine and found the spot where he'd had his little meltdown. "We'll take *and* and come up with a visual for you. That's it. It won't even be ten minutes. Just try it, okay?"

Anthony knew when somebody was trying to feed him a line of bull. And Rae wasn't. More than that, she really seemed to care if he said yes or no. It was important to her somehow. "One word," he finally agreed.

Rae jumped up and darted over to her closet. She pulled out a big plastic box and an old sheet. She spread the sheet on the floor, then sat down with the box in front of her. "We'll use clay," she said as she opened the box.

"Clay, yeah," Anthony repeated, as if he actually had some idea what she was talking about. He walked over to the sheet and sat down across from Rae. She gave him a lump of yellow modeling clay and took a lump of blue clay for herself. "Make a hand," she instructed. "Doesn't matter how good it is."

You can do that, Anthony told himself. About a minute later he had something that looked pretty much like a hand. Close enough, anyway. He wanted this whole deal over with. "Now what?" he asked Rae.

She quickly finished up the last two clay fingers she'd been working on. "Now you take your hand and my hand—" She passed him the blue clay hand she'd made. It had wrinkles and knuckles and everything, even a ring on one finger. "And you link them together so they're hand *and* hand. Keep the word *and* in your head as you connect them."

Anthony obediently joined the hands by smushing the clay fingers together. And, he thought. And, and, and, and, and.

"So hopefully, next time you see the word *and,* you'll get an image of the clay hands, and that—"

Rae was interrupted by the phone ringing. Anthony snatched it up. "Gregg?" he burst out, then he nodded at Rae to let her know it was Gregg. "Remember that guy we met at that party a couple of months ago, Frank something? Brown hair. Tattoo of a scorpion on his hand."

"With the girl in the Daisy Dukes?" Gregg asked.

"Yeah! Yeah! Him," Anthony exclaimed. "Do you know where he lives?"

Gregg hesitated for so long, Anthony wanted to reach through the phone and strangle him.

"Dude, he lives right next door to the house where the party was. That's why he was there," Gregg finally said.

"Thanks." Anthony hung up without saying good-bye. "Ready to roll?" he asked Rae.

"Always," she said, snagging her jacket off her desk chair. "Dad, we decided to go out and grab some food," Rae called as she led the way back to the front door.

"Bring your cell," he called back.

"He likes to be able to be in touch all the time since I got out of the hospital," Rae explained as they headed to the car.

"That's cool," Anthony answered. He could almost feel his blood slamming through his veins as he got behind the wheel and pulled back onto the street. They were getting close now. Very close. Maybe they'd even have Jesse back by the end of the night.

Even though I'm not good at reading, I'm good with directions, Anthony thought. He'd only been to the house where the party was one time, but he remembered exactly where it was. He didn't even have to think about how to get there. He just drove. Fifteen minutes later he was pulling into a parking spot about a block away from the place. He figured he shouldn't have his car exposed, just in case.

"What do you think?" he asked as they got out. "The one on the left or the one on the right? All Gregg said was next door."

"Let's go right. Right for Rae," she answered. It was her usual confident tone, but he could hear a slight shake in her voice. "So, do we have a plan here? Or are we just going to say, 'Hi, we know you have Jesse. Give him back'?" she asked.

"First we're going to make sure the guy even lives in one of these houses," Anthony answered. "Gregg isn't always that clear about stuff. If Frank's home, I'll give him some bull about hearing there was a party at his place. That should get us inside. You can do your fingerprint thing. If we find out Jesse's there, we call in an anonymous tip to the police. Jesse's mom's already filed a missing persons, so they'll know they should be looking for him."

"Okay. A plan. Good," Rae said as they cut across the front yard, maneuvering around the toys lying all over the place. When they reached the front porch, Anthony tilted his head from side to side, cracking his neck, then rang the doorbell. *This is it,* he thought when a woman answered the door, only opening it

144

halfway. She was wearing an old terry cloth robe with big stars on it, but she'd definitely been the one in the Daisy Dukes at the party.

"Hey, I heard you and Frank were having a blowout over here. But it looks like I got the wrong night," Anthony said.

"Yeah," the woman answered. That was it. Just yeah. *Thanks for being so freakin' friendly,* Anthony thought. Man, she was clutching the edge of the door as if he and Rae were about to storm the place.

"Is Frank around? Since we're here, might as well say hi," Anthony continued.

"No, he's working late," she said. "Look, my little boy has a fever. I have to go check on him. Call first next time, okay?" She shut the door, and Anthony heard it lock.

"Well, that was informative," he muttered.

"Let me try," Rae said. She ran her fingers over the side of the door, biting her lip in concentration. "She was lying," Rae said. "She has no idea where Frank is. He's been gone for more than a week, hasn't called or anything. She's afraid he's gotten himself into some kind of trouble again."

"So our guy has been gone for pretty much the same amount of time Jesse has," Anthony commented.

Rae ran her fingers over the doorknob and grimaced. "What?" Anthony demanded.

"Sticky," she answered. She sniffed her fingers. "Grape jelly. From the little boy, I guess. Blocked out any thoughts I might have gotten." She dug around in her purse, found a tissue, and wiped her fingers. Anthony would have just used the side of his jeans. "If I'm going to get any more, we'd have to get inside."

"That's not going to happen. At least not tonight," Anthony said. "If we stay out here on the porch too long, she's probably going to call the cops. Come on."

"I guess I can put the Mush back on my fingers," Rae said as they headed to the car. When she got there, she gave the door handle a quick wipe with her sleeve, then pulled it open. "Oh God," she whispered.

Anthony was back around to her side of the car in half a second. He had to pull her away so he could see what she was staring at. When he saw it, his body went cold.

A knife. A knife plunged deep into the back of the passenger seat. None of the blade was visible, only the shiny red handle.

The sour taste of bile crept up Anthony's throat. "I think I recognize that knife," he managed to get out. "I think it's Jesse's Swiss Army. It was a birthday present."

"So . . . so whoever has Jesse—Frank or whoever—must have put it there. Like as a message to stay away," Rae said.

They'd been up at the house for only a few minutes. That meant whoever did this was probably still very close. Anthony scanned the street. It was empty. At least it looked empty. But that didn't mean someone wasn't watching them right now. "Let's get out of here." He wanted Rae somewhere safe, somewhere where he had a better chance of protecting her.

"One second," Rae said. She reached out, fingers trembling, and touched the hilt of the knife.

In the dim glow of the closest streetlight Anthony could see her face turn pale. Even her lips lost their color. A shudder rippled through her body, then she slowly pulled her hand away.

"The thoughts are all from Jesse," she told Anthony, her voice trembling. "He's being held in some kind of warehouse. He thinks it's about a half an hour from the skateboard place in Little Five Points. He can hear the trains from where he is. And sometimes—" Her voice caught. "Sometimes there's a smell of tar." She swallowed hard. "Anthony, he has three guards on him. And they have guns."

Chapter 10

I've been watching you, Rae. That's part of the game. And I've noticed something about you. Sometimes you open doors with your elbow, and you use your sleeve to polish things before you touch them. I find this interesting. Pathetic, but interesting.

I think your power is connected to the sense of touch. I haven't figured out exactly how it works. But I'm hoping the little surprise I left you will start making it clear. I'm hoping it will make our game more fun, too. Has anyone ever told you you're not very fun, Rae? You should work on that. If you end up having the time.

* * *

Rae sat at the kitchen table, a mug of hot chocolate cradled in her hands. She didn't really feel like drinking it, but the warmth was comforting. She glanced at the clock on the microwave. After eleven. But Rae couldn't even imagine falling asleep. *I bet Anthony's still awake, too,* she thought.

She hesitated a moment, then stood up, grabbed the cordless phone off the wall mount—and realized she didn't know Anthony's number. Even with everything they'd gone through together, she'd never called him at home. Never even been to his house. Anthony was very . . . compartmentalized. Rae hesitated again. But she really needed to talk. And Anthony was the only one she could talk to right now.

Yana had called before, and Rae'd told her some of what was going on. Yana, being Yana, had immediately volunteered to help them look for the warehouse the next day. And it had helped. It had helped a lot. But Rae still couldn't sleep. Her mind was whirling with questions.

Oh, just do it, she ordered herself. She punched in 411, got Anthony's number, and called. *I'll just let it ring three times,* she promised herself. She didn't have to wait that long. Anthony picked up on the first one.

"I just keep thinking about the knife," Rae blurted out. "I know I'm the one that said it was a warning for us to mind our own business. But now—I don't know. I just don't know. Maybe someone else knows what I can do. Maybe the info from the knife is going to lead us into some kind of trap." Rae drew in a deep, shuddering breath.

"Can I talk now?" Anthony asked.

The sound of his voice was better than the hot chocolate. Much more calming. Rae sat back down. "Please. Talk."

"I've been thinking all the same stuff," Anthony admitted. "And I'm as confused as you are. One thing's for sure—that feeling you've had of being followed is on target. We were only away from the car for a few minutes. Somebody had to have the knife on them. And they had to have been waiting for the chance to leave it for us."

"Frank?" Rae asked.

"Maybe," Anthony answered.

Neither of them said anything for a long moment. "When you said you'd been thinking the same stuff I've been thinking," Rae finally said, "did you mean the part about someone knowing about my fingerprint thing?" She stood back up and started pacing around the kitchen.

"Yeah," Anthony said. "I did think about it. Because all those stories we got in Little Five Points . . . that's too random just to be—"

"People's bad memories or—I can't even think of anything else," Rae interrupted. She crossed over to the kitchen door and made sure it was locked. She'd checked it so often, she was wearing the Mush off her fingers.

"I can't think of anything else, either," Anthony admitted. "Even though it's freakin' bizarre, some-body had to have done something to those people. Which I guess means they have some kind of, uh, ability, too."

"And that someone, that someone who has pow-ers, they know the truth about me," Rae said. She checked the lock on the kitchen window.

Anthony let out a sigh. "Seems that way. Or maybe they just did it to confuse anyone who would be asking about Jesse. Even if you hadn't been able to check out what they were really thinking, it would have gotten us—or anyone else—totally off track."

"Oh God, I'm so confused." Rae groaned. She felt like her skull was too small for her brain, like the bone was pushing down so hard, it was causing thought malfunctions. "If someone knows the truth about me—then they'd know I'd get info from the knife. So why leave it unless they wanted to . . . to lure us someplace?"

"It's the best reason I can think of," Anthony said. "*If* they know about you."

"And . . . and the best reason I can think of to try and get us to some deserted warehouse is because it would be a great place for someone to try and kill me again," Rae blurted out.

Anthony was silent for a moment. "I think it

would be better—safer—if I look for the warehouse myself," he began. Rae winced. He wasn't telling her she was wrong. "Tomorrow I'll—"

"I'm going," Rae interrupted. "Trap. Warning. Assassination plot. Whatever the deal is, I'm going. We're getting Jesse back, together."

Anthony cruised slowly down the dark, empty street. "Anyplace around here would fit what we got from Jesse," he said.

"We're close enough to the tracks to hear trains. We're about a half hour from the skateboard place. And they've been doing repairs a few streets over, so Jesse could have smelled tar."

"Thanks for the recap," Yana teased. "I think I missed something when—oh, wait. I've been here the whole time."

Anthony shot her a dirty look, but Rae didn't mind having someone around who was attempting to lighten the mood a little. It wasn't that Rae didn't care what happened to Jesse or that she'd magically forgotten that she could be walking into a trap. All the nerves in her body felt like they'd had a curling iron used on them until they were singed. Having Yana around just made the stress almost bearable.

Anthony turned right. "Why this way?" Rae asked. So far Anthony'd been completely methodical, going down each street until they were two miles away from the skateboard shop, then turning down the next street and going all the way back to the street the shop was on. Now he'd suddenly changed his pattern.

"I just remembered there's an old fire station a couple of blocks over," he answered. "When I was around seven, one of my mom's boyfriends used to work there. She has this fireman thing. Anyway, he brought me there a couple of times. It's big enough that it might seem like a warehouse to Jesse, and it closed down more than six years ago when they built a new station on Meridian."

"Definitely sounds worth checking out," Rae said.

"A thing for firemen, huh? Your mom sounds cool," Yana added.

Anthony just snorted in response. He made a left and parked the car. It wasn't hard for him to find a spot. They were almost the only ones around. There were a couple of teenage guys drinking beers out of paper bags on the corner, and that was it.

"So what now? Do we try and look inside?" Yana asked.

"We wait. We watch," Anthony answered. "If this is the right place, there are guys with guns in there."

"I don't get how Jesse was even able to call you guys with that many guards," Yana said.

"Maybe they locked him in a room that somebody had accidentally left a cell phone in or something," Rae answered quickly, wanting the lie she'd told Yana to make some kind of sense. More and more, she thought Yana would be able to deal with the truth without freaking. But Rae just wasn't ready to risk it. Yana was the only real girlfriend she had. And how could she exist without one solid girlfriend to cover her back and talk bad about the guy who broke up with her?

"Probably," Anthony agreed, his eyes locked on the abandoned fire station. Rae focused her gaze on it, too, searching for a flicker of light or a fast movement in front of one of the dark windows.

"Do you think they're planning to send a ransom request to Jesse's mom?" Yana leaned her elbows on top of the front seat and propped her chin in one hand.

"Jesse's mom doesn't have any money," Anthony answered.

"So why the guys with guns?" Yana asked slowly, clearly thinking out loud. "I mean, there are lots of reasons for a kid to get snatched. But not that many for being held under an armed guard. Do you think that *whoever* could think Jesse is somebody else? Some rich brat?"

"Maybe," Rae said. "Except then wouldn't they

have already contacted the rich parents—and found out their kid was still all safe and sound at home?"

"Yeah. You're right." Yana slumped all the way back into her seat.

Rae shot a quick look over at Anthony. She was surprised he hadn't joined in the conversation. But it was like every part of his attention was on the fire station, like he didn't even realize she and Yana were in the car anymore.

"Yana, I appreciate you being here. But you're not forgetting the guns part, are you? I mean, this could end up being really dangerous," Rae said, feeling a spurt of guilt for agreeing to let Yana come with them. "If you want to bail, it's—"

"Oh, shut up," Yana said.

Rae turned around and smiled at her. "Okay," she answered. She rolled the window down a little farther, keeping the end of her sweater over her fingers since she'd decided not to wear her Mush tonight. The cool night air would help keep her awake. And maybe she'd hear something that told her someone was inside the station.

Yana followed Rae's lead, going completely silent. They all watched. They all listened. An hour went by. But they got nothing. No hint of what was going on inside. No hint if they were at all close to finding Jesse.

When another half an hour had passed, Anthony let out a growl of frustration. The sound made Rae ache inside, as if she was absorbing his pain and anger into her bones.

"What if I—" Rae began. "What if we, I mean," she corrected herself. "What if we get a little closer? Try to see in a window?"

"I say we go for it," Yana agreed. "If the guards were keeping tabs on the street, I think we'd have seen *something.*"

Anthony hesitated, then he opened his door, got out, and closed it with a soft click. He started toward the station. A second later Rae and Yana were right behind him.

"I'll take those," Rae whispered, nodding toward the windows set in the huge sliding doors. She didn't care that much about looking in. She wanted to get her fingers working. But when she touched the metal door handles, all she got was static. The fingerprints were so old and coated with grime that she couldn't even pick out a word. *There has to be a smaller door,* she thought.

She started around the building, keeping her shoulder close to the wall so she'd be harder to see. No use making herself an easy target if someone was waiting here to try and kill her.

Yes. There was another door on the other side of

the station, a door that looked like it went to an office or something. *Please, please, please,* Rae thought as she reached for the doorknob. *Give me something here.* But all she got was more static.

"Anything?" Anthony asked softly from behind her.

Rae's heart slammed into her ribs. She hadn't even realized he was there. "Nothing," she answered. "From what I've gotten so far, no one's been in here for a long time."

"Hey, guys. There's a door that's been busted open in the back," Yana said breathlessly as she hurried up to them.

"Show us," Anthony ordered.

Rae positioned every foot carefully as they crept to the back of the station. She got to the door first and did a fingerprint sweep.

/cold/*why didn't I*/no one knows/

The thoughts came through sort of fuzzy with a layer of static underneath. Rae didn't think it was very likely that the people who left them were still inside. Although if whoever took Jesse knew Rae's powers, they would know not to leave any fresh prints.

She pushed open the door. What choice did she have? Anthony managed to beat her through it. Then he just stood there, blocking it.

"What? What do you see?" Rae whispered. She

gave him a hard poke in the back when he didn't answer immediately.

"Nothing," Anthony answered. "It's empty." He stepped the rest of the way inside, then led them on a top-to-bottom search. It was useless. The whole place was empty, empty and coated with an even layer of dust. No one had been inside for a very long time. They weren't going to get Jesse back that night.

Chapter 11

Down to the final five, Anthony told himself. He forced his eyes away from the clock. He'd managed to make it almost all the way through English without getting called on, but if Goyer caught him clock watching, she'd definitely nail him. He tilted his head toward Kelly Middleton, as if he didn't want to miss even one word of what she was reading.

Anthony thought he was putting on a good show. But as soon as Kelly managed to get out the last word on the page, Goyer called on him. *At least it won't be like reading in front of Rae,* Anthony thought. *It's not like anyone in here is even listening, except Goyer, and she's completely used to Bluebirds.* He turned the page and put his finger under the first word of the sentence at the top. Nothing came into his head. He narrowed his eyes, trying to block out everything but the page in front of him. "Wh—" He sucked in a breath, tried again. "When."

"Yes," Goyer said softly.

"When," Anthony repeated. He moved his finger under the next word. He got blank head again. Crap. *Come on,* he thought. *You know this one. It's one of the easy, little ones.* A rushing sound filled his ears as he stared at the tiny word. "The," he burst out. He shoved his finger over to the next word. An image of Noah's ark filled his brain—"animal." An image of Carl, Danny, Anna, his mom, and his stepdad appeared—"family." An image of a pair of linked clay hands appeared—"and."

Suddenly Anthony felt like he'd been sucking on helium or something, like any second his body would start floating toward the ceiling. The word *and* had just popped out of his mouth. That had never happened before. He always got stuck on that one. Always.

I owe Rae another one, he thought. *Maybe with that book of hers . . . maybe with her helping me . . . maybe I won't be a freakin' moron for the rest of my freakin' life.*

Rae hurried toward the back exit of the school. She knew Anthony was probably already out in the parking lot, waiting for her, getting more pissed off by the second. It was like even breathing the air around Sanderson Prep gave him mad cow disease. Just as she started to elbow open the closest half of the big double doors, Rae felt someone give her a quick tap on the shoulder. She glanced back—and saw the person she least wanted to see. Okay, maybe there were one or two people lower on her list, but Dori Hernandez was right down there.

"What?" Rae snapped, then immediately felt a pang of guilt. Snapping at Dori was like telling Bambi he was a bad, bad little deer. She was pretty much the nicest, sweetest girl in school.

"I just wanted to ask you . . ." Dori's words trailed off, and she gave Rae a helpless look. Like she wished Rae would take over and just read her mind. Ha. If she only knew.

"What, Dori?" Rae asked, managing to keep all but a tinge of snappishness out of her tone this time. "I'm kind of in a hurry." *And I kind of wish you were dead,* she added silently. Not that she wanted Marcus back. After the way he'd treated her? No chance. But it still wasn't a laugh riot trying to be polite to the nice, nice, nice—and way too beautiful—girl that had taken Rae's place.

"I don't know how to say this," Dori confessed, giving Rae the pleading face again. "But I have to ask you. I need to know . . . really, I want the truth—"

"You're going to have to give me a little more to go on here," Rae told her. She glanced at her watch. Anthony was probably already at the mooing stage.

"Okay, you're right. Here's the thing. Last night Marcus and I were, you know, fooling around," Dori began, hesitating between practically every word.

I do not want to be hearing this, Rae thought. *Isn't it enough that Jesse's gone? Isn't it enough that I could be walking into a death trap in a couple of hours?*

"When we were right in the middle of it, he . . ." Dori gave her a sad look, big brown eyes getting a sheen of tears. Rae felt like shaking her. "Marcus called me your name," Dori continued in a rush. "And I really, really, really need to know if anything is going on between the two of you. I won't be mad at you if there is. But I need to know. Or I'm going to go crazy." Dori gave a horrified little gasp, and a blush colored her cheeks. "I'm sorry. I'm really sorry. I didn't mean it."

"It's okay to use the word *crazy* in front of me," Rae mumbled, on complete autopilot. Marcus had called Dori by *her* name. What was that about? Rae flashed on their encounter in the library, the one where she'd thought Marcus wanted to cop an easy feel in the stacks. Had he been thinking of more than that? Could he possibly be hoping to get back together with her?

"You haven't answered the question," Dori said, her eyes getting even wetter. "Which I guess is kind of an answer."

"I've hardly even talked to Marcus since I got back from the—since school started," Rae told Dori. "Next time he does that—if there even is a next time—just, I don't know, hit him over the head with a rolled-up newspaper."

Dori gave a choked laugh, then reached out and squeezed Rae's arm. "Thanks. Thanks so much. I've been wanting to talk to you for a long time, to tell you that I didn't go after Marcus or anything. I mean, he told me that you two were about to break up before you went . . . before school ended last year."

That was a big, fat lie. But Rae didn't bother to set Dori straight. Why? It wasn't her fault that Marcus was scum. "Look, I really have to go," Rae said. "And I don't think you stole Marcus from me or anything. He has a mind of his own."

Rae turned and rushed out the door. She spotted Anthony's car almost immediately and bolted toward it. "Get me away from here," she said as she climbed in, the Mush keeping her from getting thoughts off the door handle.

"Bad day, dear?" Anthony asked sarcastically. "What happened? Was someone wearing the exact same outfit?"

"I knew you'd be in a pissy mood," Rae shot back. "Come on. Let's go." Anthony was backing up before the words left her mouth. He maneuvered the car out of the parking lot and then headed in the direction of Little Five Points.

"I asked around at school, and one of the guys said there's an empty warehouse a couple of blocks behind that strip mall with the really bad pizza place. You know the one—GGs?"

"Is that a half hour away from the skateboard place?" Rae asked.

Anthony shook his head. "Not quite. But I figured maybe they didn't take Jesse straight there. Maybe they drove around a while to confuse him." He rolled his window halfway down. "Was something wrong before?" He rolled the window a little lower. "You actually did look kind of upset."

"My old boyfriend's new girlfriend just wanted to know if I was still fooling around with him. And that just puts a cherry on top of any day, don't ya think?" Rae answered.

"So, are you?" Anthony asked, eyes locked on the road in front of them.

How could he even ask her that? "Anthony

Fascinelli, come on down!" she exclaimed. "You're the lucky grand-prize winner on *Get a Clue!*"

He glanced over at her, one eyebrow raised. "I guess that's a no."

"The guy dumped me when I was in a mental hospital," Rae reminded him. "And he didn't even bother to tell me. He just let me find out on my first day back at school."

"People get back together sometimes," Anthony answered. "You don't have to act like I'm a total idiot."

For one instant Rae flashed on what it would be like to be with Marcus again. She'd get to feel Marcus's hands on her again, feel his mouth—

You're the grand-prize winner on Get a Clue, *not Anthony,* she told herself, not allowing her imagination to take the picture of her and Marcus back together any farther. It was pointless. Ridiculous. Hopeless.

It was also a lot more fun than thinking about what was really going on in her life, about what could happen if she and Anthony did find the right warehouse. But that was where she needed to keep her focus. She needed to stay sharp. Alert. Her life could depend on it. So could Jesse's.

Rae pulled a Kleenex out of her purse and wiped the Mush off her fingers. This was a situation where she was going to need all the help she could get.

"I wonder how Yana's doing with the history partner from the pits of hell today. Yana said the girl was going to chain her to a library chair until—"

"Does that car look familiar to you?" Anthony interrupted. "The blue Dodge that's two cars back?"

Rae turned around and peered at the car. "I don't know. I'm not a car person. One blue car is pretty much like another blue car."

"You've got to start paying more attention," Anthony snapped. "I think I saw that car when I was driving you home yesterday." He abruptly pulled over to the curb. "Yeah, that's it," he said when the car passed them. "I remember the orange bumper sticker."

"So do you think it's—following me?" Rae asked, watching the car until it was out of sight.

"I don't know," Anthony answered. "But we can't ignore stuff like this. We both have to really look at what's going on around us. So let's not talk, all right? Let's just keep our eyes open."

Rae nodded. It had been stupid of her to get so caught up in the Marcus-and-Dori sitch. As Anthony drove, Rae made a point of studying the cars and people around them. She hardly allowed herself to blink.

Her eyes were burning from the effort of keeping watch when Anthony parked about half a block down from a beat-looking warehouse about twice as big as the fire station. "That's it," he announced.

Rae scooted down in her seat, settling in for a bunch of hours of staring at a building. About forty-five minutes into the stakeout Anthony broke the silence.

"That thing we did, with the clay, it worked," he admitted.

"Oh God!" Rae exclaimed. "Why didn't you tell me? That's so great."

"I read the word *and*. It's not that exciting," Anthony muttered.

Rae slapped him on the side of the head. "It *is* exciting," she told him. Then she gave him another slap. "Admit it."

"Okay, okay. It's sort of cool," Anthony said, a wide smile—a little shy, a little proud, and a little embarrassed all at once—breaking across his face.

"So, we're going to keep working on it, right?" Rae asked.

"Right," Anthony answered. "And thanks. Thanks for not letting me get out of it."

"You know what? There's something we could do right now," Rae told him. "This other book I found said that it helps if you use other senses when you're having trouble with words. So lean forward a little. Actually, it would probably be better if you rested your head on the steering wheel." Rae pulled a couple of books and a binder out of her backpack.

/got to reread the/ tell Dad // what's Marcus/

Then she rolled it up, letting more of her old thoughts run through her head without really paying attention to them, and handed the backpack to Anthony. "You can use this as a pillow. Don't worry. I can watch the warehouse and do my part at the same time."

"Your part," Anthony repeated. He gave her a wary glance, then pressed the backpack against the steering wheel and lowered his head down to it.

"Close your eyes. Breathe deeply. Try and relax as much as possible," Rae instructed, noticing the way Anthony's hair curled against his collar.

"It would be easier if I knew what we were doing," Anthony said.

"I'm just going to use my finger to write some words on your back. You don't have to do anything except repeat the words in your head as I write them," Rae explained. She checked the warehouse. Still no sign of any activity. "Okay, we'll start with *on.*" As she spoke, she traced the word in big letters, pressing firmly. His back was warmer than she expected, even through his T-shirt, and hard with muscle. She traced the word over and over, starting right below his neck and working her way down until she could feel the waistband of his jeans under her finger. When she realized she'd somehow started staring at the wide T-shirt-covered expanse, she jerked her eyes back to the warehouse. Still nothing.

"Okay, I'm going to switch to *at* now," Rae announced. She began tracing the word in rows that went from one side of Anthony's back to the other. Anthony didn't answer. "You're not asleep, are you?" she asked.

"No," he said, his voice coming out all husky. "But maybe we should stop for a while."

"Don't worry about it. I'm watching the warehouse," Rae assured him, still writing on his back. "You just keep thinking the word *at* while I do this." She filled his back with *at*'s three times, eyes on the warehouse. No sign of life yet. Pretty soon they should probably risk getting close enough for her to do a fingerprint sweep.

"I wish I'd thought to bring some sandpaper," Rae said. "The book said different textures help, so if you used your finger to write words on a piece of sandpaper, it might make them easier to recognize when you read them. I guess having a bunch of different sensations connected to the words is good."

"Since you don't have any, maybe we should stop," Anthony said.

"Just using my finger will still—" Rae caught a flash of movement at the side of the warehouse. "Get down," she ordered. "Someone's coming."

Anthony scrunched down in his seat as Rae did the same. She watched as a man—maybe six feet with a bear build—headed away from the warehouse and over to a beige Toyota parked about a block from Anthony and Rae.

Anthony started the car. "What are we going to do?" Rae asked.

"Follow him," Anthony answered. "We get this guy and trade him for Jesse. Or at least make him tell us everything he knows about the setup inside. Where the guards are. If this whole thing is part of a plan to get you."

Anthony let the man get a little head start, then pulled out onto the street and began following him. "Do we have any kind of plan going here?" Rae asked, gripping the dashboard with both hands—

*Igot to get to Margarita Madness night/*NEED TO MAKE ANNA/**Barbie's hair**/

—even though Anthony wasn't speeding.

"I've got no plan until we see where he stops," Anthony answered. "I'm not going to try and run him off the road or anything."

"Probably a good decision," Rae muttered as Anthony kept on the man's tail without getting too close, heading through Little Five Points.

"He's turning left up here," Rae said, pointing toward the blinking signal.

"Yeah, I got that," Anthony answered sarcastically. He got into the left lane. "I wish there was at least a car between us here," he commented as the man's Toyota pulled out into the intersection.

"Wait. He's doing a U-y," Rae cried. But Anthony was already making a smooth U behind the Toyota.

"Good. He's stopping at that gas station," Anthony said. "That means we'll have at least a minute." He pulled into the gas station, too, and parked by the air hose, then got out and studied the tires like he was trying to decide if they needed air.

Rae watched as the man went into the minimart, then came back out with a key attached to a large piece of wood. A second later he disappeared into the men's room.

Anthony waited until the door shut behind him, then started to follow. Rae reached out and grabbed his arm, holding him tight. "You can't just go walking in there. He probably has a gun."

Anthony pulled his arm away. "Which is why the bathroom's the perfect place to go after him. He's not going to be holding his gun in there." He headed straight for the bathroom.

"Anthony, I think you should wait," Rae called after him. He didn't even glance back at her.

Chapter 12

Anthony forced himself to wait for a fifteen count before he stepped into the bathroom. Luckily the guy hadn't let the door close all the way, so the lock hadn't caught. Immediately he spotted the guy in front of the last urinal in the row. He'd just about finished zipping himself up. Perfect. Anthony lunged at him and tackled him low, slamming him to the floor. He planted one knee in the man's chest, pinning him.

"Tell me everything you know about Jesse Beven," Anthony ordered. The man didn't answer— at least not fast enough. Anthony ground his knee harder into his chest. "Talk," he ordered.

"I don't know . . . what are you talking about?" the man choked out, sounding sort of dazed.

Very smart, Fascinelli, Anthony thought as he frisked the guy, finding nothing. *Yeah, cut off his air,* then *ask him a question.* He lowered his knee a little and dug it into the man's soft gut. The little jab of pain might clear his head. "The kid you snatched. Jesse. I want to hear everything from the beginning."

"You got the wrong guy," the man wheezed, a string of saliva dripping out of the corner of his mouth.

"I got all night, buddy," Anthony told him, staring the man in the eye. He heard the bathroom door open wider and jerked his head toward the sound. Rae stood in the doorway. "I don't want you in here. Leave!" Anthony barked.

Of course, Rae didn't listen. "There are easier ways to get information," she told Anthony as she made straight for the man and knelt beside him. Anthony's stomach seized up as Rae pressed her fingertips against the scum bucket's. Her face went blank for an instant, then a series of expressions crossed her face so quickly, he could hardly identify them. Fear, greed, malice, joy.

And then horror, horror as Rae ripped her fingers away. "Tie him up," she ordered. "I don't want him to be able to move."

Anthony didn't have to be asked twice. He yanked off his belt, then straddled the man and used the belt to tie his feet together. The man gave a weak-ass buck, but he didn't have a chance of getting Anthony off him.

"Hurry," Rae urged, sounding seriously freaked out.

"What's the deal? Where's Jesse?" Anthony asked her.

"He doesn't have anything to do with Jesse. Just get him restrained and let's get out of here. Then I'll tell you everything," Rae answered.

Anthony jerked the man over onto his side, then pushed him onto his stomach and pulled his wrists together behind his back. The man started trying to fight again, so Anthony had to give his head a light rap against the cement. That kept the man quiet until Anthony had used the guy's belt to get his hands tied together as tightly as his feet.

"Let's go, let's go," Rae cried.

Anthony climbed off the man, leaped to his feet, and rushed out of the bathroom, Rae right behind him. He slammed the bathroom door shut, then spun to face her. "Okay, what?"

"The guy is part of a group using the warehouse as a crystal meth kitchen," Rae burst out. "One screwup and they could demolish half the neighborhood."

"I'll call the cops. Tell them where to find our friend and the kitchen," Anthony said. He spotted a phone booth, one of the old Superman-changing-room kind, and rushed over. This problem at least he could deal with. But the Jesse situation . . . the Rae situation . . . Anthony wasn't going to lie to himself. He was in way over his head.

When he'd finished the call, he headed back over to Rae. "I guess we need to find another warehouse. You up for more driving around, or—"

"Let's go," Rae answered. They both climbed into the car.

"We covered most of the area to the west of Little Five Points, so I figured we'd just start driving up and down the streets to the east," Anthony said.

"I'll keep doing car watch," Rae answered.

Anthony settled into a slow, methodical search. Up one street for half an hour, back down the next one. Up and down. Up and down.

"You're not going to believe this," Rae burst out. "Our friend in the blue Dodge just drove by."

Rae jerked straight up in bed, her breath coming in harsh pants. She stared wildly around her room, half expecting to see . . . she wasn't even sure what. The dream had been horrendous, but it had faded so fast that all she was left with was the sensation of someone—or something—coming after her. "You're okay," she muttered. But there was no way she was lying back down and closing her eyes. Not when that dream could be lurking.

She climbed out of bed and pulled on her robe, then glanced at the clock. Quarter to one. She'd hardly been asleep any time at all, even though the dream had felt endless.

Rae pushed a few curly strands of hair away from her face, sat down in front of her computer, and hit the power button. She needed some kind of mindless game to distract her. All she could think about was that blue Dodge—who was in it? Who was following her and Anthony? They'd tried to go after the car when she'd spotted it, but Anthony had lost it after a few blocks of heavy traffic. So if the driver really *was* tracking her, he or she was still out there somewhere. . . .

Rae shook her head, then clicked on the icon for solitaire. But before she could start playing, the phone rang. She snatched it up. "Hello?"

"It's Anthony."

His tone made the little hairs on her arms stand straight up.

"What? What happened?" she demanded.

"It's not that big of a deal," he answered. "It's just—I took my car over to this place after I dropped you at home, where I've done some work for extra cash. I wanted my friend to check things out, see if he could get a handle on how that blue Dodge kept finding us." He paused, and Rae pressed her lips together, afraid of what was coming. "He found a bug in the car," Anthony finished.

"And that's no big deal?" Rae exclaimed.

"We already knew we were being followed," Anthony said. "We just didn't know high-tech equipment was involved. Anyway, I got rid of it. And now I'll be looking for more, so that will make it a little harder on the Dodge guy."

"Whoever that is," Rae said.

"Yeah. Well, I just thought you should know, it's under control. I've gotta go. See you tomorrow, okay?" Anthony hung up without saying good-bye. But a second later the phone rang again.

"Anthony?" Rae said as soon as she picked it up.

There was no answer. Only a low male laugh. "Who is this?" Rae said, trying not to sound as scared as she was.

"I get it now," a voice replied. Rae instantly recognized Marcus Salkow's arrogant tone. A mixture of relief and a new kind of dread washed over her. "Rae's got herself another guy."

"Marcus, why are you calling?" Rae asked. He sounded lubricated—not off-his-butt drunk, but like he'd had a couple of beers.

"I was making out with Dori the other night, and I called her Rae," Marcus said. "I called her Rae," he repeated, as if she might have missed it the first time.

Rae opened her curtains halfway and cracked the window. She needed some air. "Why are you telling me this? This is something between you and Dori."

"Because . . ." The pause went on so long, Rae wanted to scream. "Because . . . I think I called her that because I miss you," Marcus admitted.

The confession was like a body blow. Rae didn't think she'd be able to say anything, even if she knew what she wanted to say.

"I know I really hurt you. I totally screwed up," Marcus continued. "And no matter what happens, I want you to know that I'm sorry. What I did to you . . . that's the worst thing I've ever done to anybody."

"Thanks," Rae murmured, surprised to feel tears welling up in her eyes. It was just that this was too familiar, talking to Marcus on the phone late at night. When they'd been together, they'd talked like this all the time.

"I want . . . would you want . . ." Marcus let out a frustrated sigh. "I thought maybe we could try getting back together. Whenever I see you at school . . ." He let his words fade away again.

"I don't know. I don't know if that could even be possible," Rae said in a rush. But God, it would feel so incredible to be part of Rae and Marcus again. So good. So safe.

Unless Marcus is just like Jeff Brunner. What if Dori isn't going as far as Marcus wants? What if Marcus thinks a girl like me—like I am now—would be so grateful to have him that I'd do anything he wants?

Or what if he was serious? What if he really wanted to be with her again? What if he really did miss her? Would he be able to take the stares? Because people would definitely stare if they got back together. Yeah, they'd be more subtle about it. And yeah, Marcus's friends would be cool because whatever Marcus did was okay with them.

But he still might not be able to handle going out with the school freak. He might just bolt again, and that . . . she might not recover from that.

"Rae?" Marcus finally said.

"I don't . . . this isn't something I can say yes or no to right now," Rae answered. "I have to go."

"Wait. Wait. I just want to play you this one song first," Marcus said. Rae heard a button click, and the song that was on the radio the first time Marcus kissed her began to play. It took her right back to that moment. They were sitting in his car, parked outside her house. She'd known he was going to kiss her, and as each minute ticked by that he *didn't,* it was like the air got more and more charged with electricity. When his lips finally touched hers, the kiss swept through her entire body.

I can't listen to this, Rae thought. The song wasn't even half over, and she was going to burst into tears any second. *I can't deal with this right now. Not with everything else that's going on in my life. After we get Jesse back, then I'll think about Marcus.*

Anthony felt someone poke his arm. He slitted open his eyes. There was no light outside his window. The sky hadn't even lightened to gray yet. He rolled onto his side. "Way too early," he mumbled. He got another poke on the arm. Reluctantly he opened his eyes all the way and sat up. Anna stood next to him.

"I wet the bed," she said, staring down at the floor.

"Why are you telling me about it?" Anthony asked, still half asleep. "You have a mother."

Anna backed up a couple of steps. "Tom might wake up, too."

"All right, all right," Anthony muttered. He climbed out of bed. It wasn't that Tom was some kind of wicked stepfather. But the guy did have a mouth on him sometimes, and he knew exactly what to say to make any of them feel about an inch and a half tall. And as he got a good look at Anna's face, he realized that she was already feeling like a total loser. She kept biting her lip, probably to avoid bawling, and her eyes were darting around like she was scared somebody was going to see her.

Anthony grabbed a pair of sweatpants off the floor and pulled them on over his boxers. "Okay, this is no big deal. I'm going to show you what to do, and next time you won't have to wake anybody up," he said as he led her back to the room she shared with Carl.

He crossed over to her dresser and fished out a new pair of pajamas. "First, get cleaned up and put these on," he told her. He checked on Carl while Anna ran to the bathroom. The kid probably wouldn't wake up if someone set off an air horn next to his head. Anthony reached out and ran one finger down Carl's cheek. It was so soft, it was hard to believe it was skin. *Wonder what it feels like to be three?* he thought.

"Okay, I'm done," Anna whispered as she slipped back into the room.

"Right. Next step, take the sheets off your bed, and put on new ones." Anthony grabbed a pair of worn sheets off the shelf inside her closet. He and Anna each took one side of the bed and got the new sheets on—about twice as slowly as it would have taken him to do it himself. But he knew if Anna was going to stop feeling like a screwup, she needed to learn how to deal with the wet bed situation on her own.

"Now what?" Anna asked. Anthony noticed she'd stopped biting her lip.

"Now we put the old sheets and pajamas in the washer. Come on. I'll show you." He took her little hand in his and led her down to the kitchen. "You turn this knob to small," he explained. "Then you put this one on hot/hot, open the lid, and stick the stuff in."

He waited while Anna followed his instructions, wondering what his sister would think if she knew how long it had taken him to memorize the stupid words for each setting on the machine. "Now put in the detergent. One capful." Anna measured the soap out like it was some kind of explosive.

"Good job," Anthony said. "Now shut the lid. Then move this big knob to regular"—he pointed to the spot on the dial—"and pull it out." He nodded as Anna got the load started. "Now first thing in the morning, you take the stuff out and put it in the dryer. All you have to do is move the knob to the thirty or forty mark, then close the dryer."

"But what if somebody gets up before me? They'll know," Anna said. Her voice had a little quiver in it.

"Look, I'm pretty wide awake, so tonight I'll stay up and put the stuff in the dryer. When it's done, I'll stick it back in your closet," Anthony told her. What else was he supposed to say? "Next time—'cause you know, it happens sometimes, which is no biggie—you can stay awake if you want. But you know how it is here in the morning. It's not like anyone's going to be checking out the dryer to see if someone was doing wash in the middle of the night."

Anna hurled herself at him, wrapping her arms tight around his waist. "Thanks." Before he could answer, she was out of the kitchen. Anthony sat down at the kitchen table. Already his eyes felt droopy. But he couldn't fall asleep. He'd told Anna the sheets and pj's would be in her room in the morning, and that was going to happen.

He glanced at the kitchen clock—one of those cat ones with the swinging tail and the eyes that rolled back and forth. Not even midnight.

By now the Dodge guy has to know his tracking device has been flushed, Anthony thought. Crap. He should have put it in another car. That would have kept the guy off their tail for—for what? Another few hours? Another day? It wouldn't take a genius to realize that he and Rae weren't in whatever car Anthony would have stuck the bug in.

And by now whoever was following them knew the basics. They had to know where Anthony lived. Where Rae lived. Where the group therapy was held. Where he went to school. Where Rae went to school.

He had a bad feeling that Jesse wasn't the only one in danger. And there was nothing he could do to keep any of them safe.

Rae sat cross-legged in the center of her bed. There was no way she could sleep now. Not after Marcus's call, and especially not after Anthony's news about the bug. Plus fear for Jesse. Fear for herself. God. She might never sleep again.

Rae leaned over and grabbed her sketch pad and a piece of charcoal off her nightstand. The charcoal instantly started moving across the paper. She was in the zone, that place where her hand felt like it had a will of its own. Her art teacher, Ms. O'Banyon, always said that Rae's best work came when she trusted the hand. Rae agreed, but it was still kind of a freaky sensation.

Figures quickly began to appear on the paper. Marcus smiling. Anthony, ready to fight. Jesse curled up in the bottom corner, half off the page. And over all of them, taking up most of the top half of the sketch, a face. Almost featureless. Except for the eyes. The eyes that seemed to see everything.

She ripped the page off the pad and crumpled it up. This was not helping. She turned off her light and crawled back under the covers, deciding to at least attempt sleep. Then she realized she'd left the curtains open.

Great. She couldn't sleep like this. Never could. She felt way too exposed. With a sigh she climbed back out of bed and started toward the window. Her heart turned to stone in her chest. Somebody was out there. She could make out a dark figure right across the street from her house. Staring at her window. They probably couldn't see her now that her light was off. But how long had they been there? What had they seen?

Rae jammed on her sneakers and pulled on a jacket. Then, without giving herself a chance to change her mind, she darted out of her room and through the house. She crept out the front door, opening it just enough to squeeze through. The person—she couldn't tell if it was a man or woman—was still there. Now what was she supposed to do?

You're supposed to find out who they are, she answered herself as she crossed the damp lawn, keeping her body low. She moved up to a parked car and crouched behind it, leaning out just enough to spy on the person who'd been spying on her. They were glancing around as if they had a feeling they were being watched. *Don't leave,* Rae silently begged. *Not until I get a good look at you.*

But the person was already starting down the street away from Rae's house, first walking, then jogging. Rae did the only thing she could think to do—she started after them. When the person broke into a sprint, Rae did, too. She ran until her chest burned and she had to gasp for every breath. God, why hadn't she ever actually tried in gym?

The person ahead of her was almost out of sight. They stumbled, fell, but quickly regained their footing and kept running until they were lost in the darkness. Rae couldn't make herself take one more step. If she did, her lungs would explode. She sank down on the cold sidewalk, feeling her frantically pounding heart slow down. This might have been her only chance to find out who was following her, and she'd blown it.

Rae pushed herself to her feet. Something white halfway down the block caught her eye. Had the person following her dropped it? Still breathing hard, Rae walked down the sidewalk. As she got closer to it, she realized the white thing was a large envelope. She picked it up, moved under the closest streetlight, and opened it.

"Oh God," she whispered. The envelope was full of pictures—pictures of Rae. In her bedroom. In her kitchen. In her living room. At school. At the institute. In Little Five Points with Anthony. All the nightmares she'd been having were more real than she could have imagined. Someone really *had* been watching her—everywhere.

Chapter 13

"**O**kay, everyone, that's it for today's session," Ms. Abramson announced. *Today's* group *session at least,* Rae thought. She still had to have a private chat with Ms. Abramson. Rae was a newbie in the group, and she hadn't been out of the hospital all that long, so she was still on the list of people needing some—gag—special attention.

"I'll meet you out in the parking lot," she told Anthony. "Abramson said it wouldn't take that long."

Anthony leaned close, a section of his brown hair brushing against her cheek. "The faster you give it up, the faster you get done," he advised.

"Ready, Rae?" Ms. Abramson asked.

Rae nodded, and Ms. Abramson led the way down to her office. *Anthony's right,* she thought as she took a seat in front of Ms. Abramson's desk. Rae was going to have to dredge up some of the ugly stuff, some of the feelings she didn't want to feel. No way was Ms. Abramson going to let her get away with saying everything was fine, fine, all fine.

"So how's life been treating you?" Ms. Abramson asked as she sat down. She reached for a cold cup of coffee, and Rae noticed there was a long, raw-looking strip that ran almost from her wrist to her elbow.

"I fell playing tennis," Ms. Abramson said, noticing the direction of Rae's gaze. "I admit it. I'm a klutz. But we're not here to talk about me."

"Stuff with my dad is going pretty well," Rae began, wanting to get this over with as quickly as possible. Every second that she and Anthony weren't out there searching for Jesse was longer that he was in danger. That they all were. "I don't think he's as worried about me," she continued, twisting her hands together in her lap. "So that makes it less tense. Before, I was always kind of stressing about him stressing about me, you know?"

Ms. Abramson nodded. "I think a lot of times parents forget that their kids worry about them almost as much as they worry about their kids," she answered. She took a sip of the coffee, grimaced, and put the cup back down. "How about school? How does it feel to be back there? I know you've talked about it some in group, but I'd like to hear more."

"Classes are good. Especially art. My teachers are still watching me pretty closely. It's like there are eyes on me everywhere," Rae said. She definitely wasn't going to tell Ms. Abramson that she was being followed. Talk about a one-way ticket to the hospital.

"School is more than classes. What about friends? Do you feel like they're watching you, too?" Ms. Abramson asked.

"Pretty much everyone is still weird around me, but I'm getting through," Rae said. She glanced at Ms. Abramson, and it was clear that she was going to have to get more detailed if she was going to satisfy the woman and get out of there. She couldn't talk about the really huge stuff in her life. Her fingerprint power. That there was someone who wanted her dead—someone who might have even kidnapped Jesse to get to her.

But there was one thing that kept creeping into her mind. And it was probably big enough to satisfy Ms. Abramson, who was just sitting there, watching Rae, waiting, obviously willing to wait all afternoon. "Um, my old boyfriend, Marcus . . . he says he wants to get back together with me."

"That's big," Ms. Abramson said, fiddling with the handle of her coffee cup. "Is it something you want?"

Rae shrugged. "I don't know. I mean, I was so happy with him, totally, completely happy. Being with Marcus was the best thing ever. But then when I was in the hospital, he moved on to another girl in, like, three seconds. Does he actually think I can trust him again after that?"

"Do you see any set of circumstances in which you *could* trust him again?" Ms. Abramson asked. She took another sip of her coffee, grimaced again, then put the cup on the bookshelf behind her.

"Maybe if he was wearing one of those collars— the ones cops put on people when they're confined to their house or whatever," Rae joked nervously. "It's like Marcus ripped a chunk out of my body and now he's saying he's sorry, like he forgot to call me when he said he would."

"Have you ever considered saying any of this to him?" Ms. Abramson asked. "It sounds like something that needs to be addressed before you can even think about whether or not you want a relationship with him again."

"I've talked to him a little," Rae said. She sighed, a sigh so deep, it hurt coming out of her lungs. "But I don't think he really gets it."

Ms. Abramson leaned across her desk toward Rae. "I don't want to be dismissive of your feelings about Marcus, but is anything else bothering you? It doesn't look to me like you've been sleeping well. There are dark smudges under your eyes, and in group you seemed to have some trouble concentrating." Ms. Abramson pinned Rae with a gaze so intense, it got Rae squirming in her chair. "Is something else going on, Rae?" Ms. Abramson pressed.

"Jesse," Rae blurted out. "I'm worried about Jesse. He's been gone so long. I keep thinking about what could have happened to him."

"Jesse," Ms. Abramson repeated. Her gaze grew even more intense, like she'd switched on the high beams or something. "That is a disturbing situation. Tell me more about how you feel when you think of Jesse."

"The idea that someone's holding him prisoner just makes me insane," Rae burst out. Immediately she realized she'd made a big mistake.

And of course, Ms. Abramson picked right up on it. "Why would you think someone's holding Jesse prisoner?" she asked, her voice coming out the slightest bit strained.

"I guess I just . . . lately I kind of imagine the worst. I don't know why. Maybe it's because I was in the hospital and saw all these people who had ended up so badly. I—I don't know," Rae stammered.

"You've gone through a lot in the past months. It's not uncommon for people in your situation to become more pessimistic." She flipped open her date book. "I only scheduled time for us to have a quick chat today, but I'm concerned that you've begun to see the world in a negative way, and I'd like to work with you on it. How about if we meet for an hour after the next group meeting?"

It was one of those adult questions that weren't really questions at all. "Sure. Okay. That would be good." Rae jumped up from her chair. "So can I go now? Someone's waiting for me."

"You can go," Ms. Abramson said. "I'm glad we'll have some more time to spend one-on-one. You have so many gifts, Rae. I want to help you to realize all the potential inside you."

"Um, thanks," Rae answered. Then she bolted. She hurried out to the parking lot and climbed into Anthony's car.

"How'd it go?" Anthony asked.

"You know . . . she wants me to be the best me I can be and blah, blah, blah." Rae opened her backpack, pulled out her binder, and flipped it open, allowing her old thoughts to rush through her head. She'd decided not to wear the Mush for a while. If she hadn't been wearing it so much, she might have touched a print that would have told her Anthony's car was bugged. She couldn't afford to miss any information right now.

"Like I told you, I went online at lunch and found a couple more buildings that fit the info we got from Jesse. I made a little map." Rae tilted the binder toward Anthony. "I think the old meat-packing place is the best bet. The other ones are farther away from where they're repairing the streets, and I'm not sure if the tar smell would reach them, although it might."

Anthony nodded, and he pulled out of Oakvale's parking lot. "Are we picking up Yana first?"

"She can't come. She called me on my cell at school. She said either she and her partner are finishing their project tonight or Yana's going to strangle the girl."

Anthony punched on the radio, and pounding techno filled the car. The beat of the music filled her body, revving her up. *We're going to find him today,* she thought. *No matter what it takes. If we have to stake out every warehouse in Atlanta, we're finding Jesse before we go home.* She tried not to let herself think about the fact that finding Jesse could mean finding the person who wanted to kill her.

"We're finding him tonight," Anthony half shouted over the music, echoing Rae's thoughts. When they were about a block away from the meat-packing factory, he killed the music, then parked as close as he could to the factory without being totally obvious. The building was set about fifty feet back from the street and surrounded by a high metal fence.

"You want to do a little work while we wait?" Rae asked. "I brought some clay."

"Okay," Anthony answered. He was actually giving it a real try. But that was Anthony. He didn't back down once he said he'd do something.

Rae pulled a Ziploc bag out of her purse—

/Anthony will/ want to try another/ maybe felt/

—and took out a couple of balls of colored clay. "What word do you want to do this time?" she asked.

"How about *on?*" Anthony asked as she handed him some of the clay.

"You could make a skateboard, and I could make Jesse. Then we could put Jesse on the skateboard," Rae suggested. Anthony gave one of his signature grunts, and they both started to work. Rae made sure to glance at the factory every few seconds. So far, it looked deserted.

After they finished the clay representation of *on,* they did one for *after*—a baby elephant holding a big elephant's tail; one for *even*—a perfectly balanced scale; and one for *what*—a girl with a question mark for a head.

"Let's stop for a while," Rae said, doing another factory check. Still nothing going on. Anthony handed her the clay, and she stuck it in the Ziploc along with hers, then jammed it back in her purse. As she pulled her hand back out, one of her silver rings hit on something hard. She felt around and realized that there was something in the inside pocket.

What would I have put in there? she wondered. She never used that pocket. She unzipped it and slid in two fingers. Almost immediately they brushed against something cool and smooth.

/never felt like I do about Rae/hope she knows/

Oh God. Rae recognized the flavor of that thought. It came from Marcus. She pulled the hard, smooth object free. It was the locket Marcus had given her on their two-month anniversary. The chain had broken a few days before The Incident. Rae'd put the locket in the little pocket for safekeeping. Then with everything that had happened, she'd forgotten about it. Gently she ran her fingers over it.

/want to be with her all the time/can't stop thinking/*think I love him*/

That last thought, the think-I-love-him one, was Rae's. It brought with it a burst of old emotion, of love so new and wonderful, it made her giddy, and of a passion that burned until she thought she'd go crazy.

Tears stung her eyes. Would she ever feel that way again? Would anyone ever feel that way about *her?* Could Marcus still actually feel that way after everything that had happened? He was so freaked out by her being hospitalized. How could he even want to look at her again?

"What's that?" Anthony asked, glancing over at her, then returning his gaze to the factory.

"Nothing," Rae said quickly.

Anthony paused, then shrugged. "We've been here a couple of hours and haven't seen anything," he said. "I think it's safe to go a little closer. At least up to the fence."

Rae climbed out of the car—

/today has to be/

—and she and Anthony walked across the street and down the sidewalk to the fence. There was a gate held closed by a thick chain and a padlock. Rae pulled in a deep breath, then ran her fingers lightly down one of the metal bars. A blast of pure terror slammed into her, knocking her heart back against her spine.

/don't make me go in there/don't/what if gun/

"What?" Anthony took Rae by the shoulders and pulled her away from the fence.

"Jesse's in there," Rae answered, rubbing her fingers against the front of her pleated pants. "At least he was. And Anthony, he's terrified."

Anthony wrapped his arm around Rae's shoulders and walked her back to the car, trying to look casual in case anybody in the factory was watching. He opened the passenger door and helped her inside. Her whole body was trembling, and it made him want to punch something. Instead he slammed the door as hard as he could, then strode around the car and got in his side. He slammed his door, too. It didn't make him feel any better.

He shoved his hands through his hair. He couldn't just sit here if Jesse was inside. "Wait here," he ordered Rae. "I'm going in."

Rae grabbed his arm with both hands. He could feel her nails, even through his jean jacket. "Are you insane? We know there are guys with guns guarding Jesse. We know this whole thing could be a trap. You can't just go strolling in."

Anthony jerked away. "I'm going." He studied the factory. "It looks like there's a skylight up there. I can climb onto that Dumpster over on the side, and from there I can make it up the fire escape to the roof. No one'll be expecting me to come in that way."

He opened his door. Rae grabbed his arm again. "If you're going, I'm going with you."

"You don't look like you could even do one pull-up. You're not going to be able to haul yourself up from the Dumpster to the fire escape." He could give her a boost, but he wasn't going to tell her that. He wanted her in the car. Safe.

Before Rae could protest, Anthony pulled away from her again and scrambled out of the car. He headed back to the gate, not going too fast. If someone was watching, he wanted them to catch him while he was still outside. He'd have a lot better chance of staying alive that way. But no one stopped him when he approached the gate again. He waited a few more seconds, then climbed over. Keeping low, glad that it was dark, he ran to the Dumpster and swung himself on top of it. One half was open, and he could see that it was empty. Whoever was inside was being careful not to leave any traces.

Anthony looked up at the fire escape over his head. The bottom rung of the ladder was almost in reach. He stood on his toes and stretched one arm up until it felt like it was about to pop out of its socket. He reached for the rung, missed it, tried again, and snagged it with two fingers. *Yes!* He gave the ladder a yank, and it came down with a rusty screech. Anthony froze, sure someone would come running to check out the sound. But the only sound was his heart pounding in his ears. No footsteps running toward him. No gunshots.

Go. Just go, he ordered himself. He started to haul himself up the ladder. It swayed under his weight, but Anthony didn't let himself think about that. He concentrated on moving up one rung at a time. When he reached the roof, he muttered a quick prayer, then crept over to the skylight. He stretched out on his stomach and pressed his face against the grimy glass. But he couldn't see anything. Too dark.

Anthony reached out and started to scrub one section of the glass with the sleeve of his jacket. He heard a faint cracking sound and saw a hairline fracture run through the glass. *Okay, okay, don't panic,* he told himself. He slowly began to slide backward. If he could just get off the skylight—

But it was too late. The glass shattered, and Anthony was falling. He hit the floor with a bone-crushing thud, then everything went black.

Chapter 14

"Oh my God," Rae gasped. She wasn't completely sure; it was almost too dark to tell, but it looked like . . . it looked like Anthony had just fallen through the skylight. She scrambled out of the car and ran down to the gate. There was no way she could climb it. Why was she such a total, pathetic weakling?

Rae's eyes darted along the fence. Maybe there was a place she could squeeze through, or . . .

Her gaze fell on the large padlock holding the gate together. When people opened combination locks, they usually thought about the numbers as they did it. "Let this work. Let this work," Rae muttered as she ran her fingers over the lock's dial.

/thirteen/twenty-seven/five/

With shaking fingers Rae dialed in the numbers she'd gotten from the fingerprints. The lock didn't open. And Anthony and Jesse were inside with who knew what happening to them. *Panicking isn't going to help,* she told herself. *Focus. Maybe you got the numbers right but the order wrong.* She shook out her hand, then tried again. Twenty-seven. Five. Thirteen.

Rae yanked down on the lock. It didn't open.

Five. Thirteen. Twenty-seven. "Please, please, please." Yank. And the lock opened with a well-oiled click. Rae pulled it off the chain, dropped it on the ground, and shoved open the gates. She didn't care who saw her. She hoped somebody did. Maybe it would create enough of a diversion to give Anthony a chance to do . . . something.

Rae raced toward the factory. She grabbed the long metal handle of the front door with both hands and tugged with all her strength.

/no one's ever gonna find me/

But it was locked. Of course it was locked. "Don't worry, Jesse," she said as she ran to the closest window. "Somebody's gonna find you right now."

There was no point in trying to be quiet anymore, so Rae jerked off her cashmere sweater, wrapped it tightly around her fist, then slammed her fist through the window. One of her fingers started to bleed, but she ignored it. She used her sweater-wrapped hand to knock away as much glass from the frame as she could.

Then she climbed into the factory.

Anthony slowly sat up, clenching his teeth so he wouldn't cry out. It felt like someone was stomping across his back in baseball cleats.

He did a quick scan of the dark room, ignoring the little explosions of light in front of his eyes. The room was huge, clearly running the length of the building. It was also empty.

But I had to make a hell of a lot of noise falling down here, Anthony thought. He wondered how long he'd been knocked out. It could have been less than a minute. But a minute was long enough for somebody to be practically on top of him. He pushed himself to his feet and listened hard. Yeah, someone was coming up the stairs. They were trying to be quiet, but he could hear the creak of the treads.

Weapon. He needed some kind of weapon. There wasn't going to be a spare gun lying around, but there had to be something he could use. Anthony spotted a pile of construction materials against the back wall. He crept over. A bunch of boards. And some bricks. He grabbed a couple of bricks as quickly as he thought he could without alerting whoever was coming for him, then he tiptoed back across the room and positioned himself just inside the doorway. He raised the bricks over his head.

Come and get me. You're going to be the one who goes down, he thought.

Rae crept up the last flight of stairs. Her footsteps echoed as if she was the only one in the factory. But she knew that there had to be others in here.

She took another step. Hesitated. She held her breath, hoping to hear the tiny sound again. But the factory stayed silent. *You've got to keep going,* she told herself. The hair on her arms began to prickle, and she got that familiar feeling, the feeling of being watched.

Oh God. Who was in here? Did they have a gun pointed at her right now? Were they waiting for her to move into the right position so they could shoot her through the head?

Rae's heart pounded so hard that the sound filled her ears.

She had only two choices. Up or down. She chose up. Took a step. Hesitated. Tried to listen. But all she could hear was the thud of her heartbeat.

Rae took another step. She peered at the open doorway at the top of the stairs. It was too dark up there to see anything. She hurled herself up the last few steps. If someone was there with a gun, at least she'd be harder to hit, she thought as she plunged through the open doorway.

Something moved in the darkness to her left. A man. She dropped to the floor and rolled. But he was too quick for her. A second later he had her shoulders pinned to the floor.

"I told you to wait in the car," he whispered furiously. Rae opened her eyes and saw it was Anthony kneeling over her. The rush of relief made her dizzy.

"I almost brained you with one of these things," Anthony said, holding up a brick. "What is the matter with you?"

"I would have waited in the car if you hadn't fallen through the roof," Rae shot back. "And you don't have to whisper. The place is deserted."

Anthony dropped both bricks. "Crap," he exploded. "They must have moved him."

Rae hadn't even thought of that. She'd been so relieved to find Anthony alive—without getting killed herself—that she'd forgotten all about Jesse for a second.

"Now we have nothing to go on. All the info you got from the knife was about this place. It's useless to us now," Anthony burst out. He slammed his fist into the wall.

Rae winced, imagining the pain. She wanted to say something reassuring, something comforting.

But he was right. They were back to square one. And the more time that passed . . . she didn't let herself complete the thought.

"Come on. Let's get out of here." She wrapped her fingers around the sleeve of his jacket, not wanting to accidentally invade his thoughts by touching his fingers, and led him down the first flight of stairs, through the next level of the factory, also empty, and down to the main level, which still had rows of meat hooks hanging from the ceiling. "Quite the decor, huh?" she muttered.

"Yeah. I—" Anthony was interrupted by a faint, rhythmic knocking. "It's coming from over there." Anthony spun to the left and ran between a row of the hooks, Rae still clinging to him. The knocking grew louder and louder. Anthony veered toward a door and yanked it open to find a small supply closet. Jesse was huddled in the back, a sponge duct taped into his mouth, wrists and ankles bound.

Rae let out a horrified cry. Anthony reached Jesse in two long strides and had him free in seconds. Then his arms were around Jesse, his cheek pressed against Jesse's head. Rae hung back, her heart aching with a mix of joy and relief and leftover fear.

Anthony and Jesse broke apart. Rae didn't know if Jesse'd want her hugging him. But she couldn't help herself. It was too good to see him. Jesse hugged her back hard, for a second, then gave her a little push away.

"What happened?" Anthony asked him. "Just start at the beginning, and don't leave anything out."

Jesse's wide grin faded. He started to sway on his feet, and Anthony reached out and steadied him. "I don't remember," Jesse said. His voice was husky, and for the first time Rae noticed how large his pupils were. *What did they do to him?* she wondered.

Rae knelt and picked up a piece of the duct tape, ran her fingers down it, and got—nothing. She checked the other pieces—nothing. "They must have been wearing gloves," she murmured. She checked the skin of Jesse's arms, the doorknob of the closet, the roll of duct tape she spotted on a shelf. "I'm not getting anything at all."

"Then let's get out of here," Anthony said.

Jesse took a step toward the door, and his knees buckled. "My legs are kind of numb."

Anthony didn't say anything. He just looped one arm around Jesse's shoulders. Rae positioned herself on Jesse's other side and wrapped one arm around his waist. Together she and Anthony half carried Jesse out of the warehouse and down to the car. They eased him into the backseat, and Rae climbed in beside him. "There's some soda in my backpack," she told Anthony.

He pulled out a can, popped the top, and handed it to Jesse. Jesse took a long pull, then started to choke. "Easy, easy," Rae said.

"It was a test. A test for you," Jesse blurted out.

"Who told you that?" Anthony asked, and Rae could tell he was struggling to keep his voice calm.

"I don't remember," Jesse answered. He rubbed his forehead with both hands. "My head feels like it's getting stabbed with ice picks."

Anthony started the car. "We're going to get you home to your mom. Then we'll call a doctor."

"Can I touch your fingertips?" Rae asked. "I know you're still shaky, but maybe you still have some memories there that I can reach, and we can find out who did this to you."

Jesse held out his hands, and Rae took them in her own, carefully matching up their fingertips. The emotions and memories hit her like a punch. Fury over a woman—Jesse's mother—being beaten. Exhilaration at making an impossible skateboard jump. An oily mix of pleasure and guilt as a fire spread out of control. Faster and faster the memories came. Thoughts and emotions almost too quick to connect to each other, overlapping as they sped through her brain. Then clear as an announcement over a loudspeaker, she got a thought all by itself—*a test for Rae.*

She dropped Jesse's hands. "He's right," she

whispered. "It was a test for me. But I don't know what kind of test, or why, or who was doing the testing." She shook her head. "At least it wasn't a trap. Or not the kind we thought."

"This is screwed up," Anthony exploded. "I don't understand it."

"It was all about me," Rae told them. "That much is very clear. It had nothing to do with Jesse. Whoever did this was just using him to find out something about me." Hot bile splashed against the back of her throat. She swallowed hard and felt it burn all the way down.

"It's okay," Jesse said.

"No, it's not okay!" Rae burst out. "You both have to stay away from me. Somebody was willing to risk Jesse's life to find out something about me. Somebody else—or maybe the same person—tried to kill me. This has nothing to do with the two of you. Just drop me off. I'll find my own way home."

"You didn't have any problem putting yourself at risk to get Jesse back," Anthony snapped, glaring at her in the rearview mirror. "We wouldn't do any less for you. If you think we would, you're the friggin' moron."

"Yeah," Jesse agreed. "This isn't over until we find the creeps who did it. All three of us."

"All three of us," Anthony repeated.

Rae looked from Anthony to Jesse. They meant it. She nodded. "All three of us," she agreed.

* * *

Our game is over, Rae, at least the first round. And I won. I found out what I wanted to know. If you touch something, you can get the thoughts of the person who held it. That's how you found the factory. You got the thoughts I implanted in Jesse's brain when you touched the knife I sent.

Jesse knows who I am. He knows everything. At least he used to. But I can extract thoughts as well as implant them, and I cleaned your friend's mind before I left him in the factory.

Now what to do? Your power isn't dangerous—unless you have an ability that I haven't discovered. But you're an interesting girl, Rae. I think I'll watch you a little longer, maybe play another round or two. Especially if it means I can find out who else is interested in you. I know about him, Rae—the person following you, taking pictures of you. I don't know who he is, but I know he's out there. And before you and I play again, I need to learn more about your other enemy—the one who must have been responsible for that pitiful pipe bomb attempt.

But you will have to pay eventually. Don't think I'll forget about my revenge. You don't deserve your perfect little life. And you aren't going to get to keep it.